P9-BZG-883

Praise for the novels of Charlotte Hughes

What Looks Like Crazy

"With her trademark characters, Hughes pens a fast-moving story about a shrink whose life careens from dealing with patients to coping with family . . . a fun formula."   —*Romantic Times*

"You cannot go wrong with Charlotte Hughes's *What Looks Like Crazy*."   —*NovelTalk*

"Absolutely hilarious! . . . Quirky . . . thought provoking . . . I am hoping for a sequel!"
          —*The Romance Readers Connection*

Hot Shot

"A tough-talking, in-your-face heroine . . . romantic comedy at its best."
          —Janet Evanovich, *New York Times* bestselling author

"One of the best books of the year . . . every wonderful character created by Charlotte Hughes is outstanding."
          —*Affaire de Coeur* (five stars)

"A delightful read with very real characters readers can relate to and root for."   —*Romantic Times*

A New Attitude

"An appealing romance filled with charm and snappy dialogue."   —*Booklist*

"With well-crafted characters and delightful banter, this is just plain fun!"   —*Romantic Times*

continued . . .

Valley of the Shadow

"Hughes's snappy dialogue and strong writing aptly describe the small Southern town and its attitude toward a girl corrupted by the big city . . . An entertaining and fast-paced murder mystery."   —*Publishers Weekly*

And After That, the Dark

"One of the Southern thrillers that never lets up and makes you unable to put it down. It's exciting enough to even give terror a good name. Charlotte Hughes is the real thing."
        —Pat Conroy, *New York Times* bestselling author

"This story and its characters will remain with you long after you've turned the last page."
        —Janet Evanovich, *New York Times* bestselling author

Jove titles by Charlotte Hughes

WHAT LOOKS LIKE CRAZY
NUTCASE

NUTCASE

Charlotte Hughes

JOVE BOOKS, NEW YORK

THE BERKLEY PUBLISHING GROUP
Published by the Penguin Group
Penguin Group (USA) Inc.
375 Hudson Street, New York, New York 10014, USA
Penguin Group (Canada), 90 Eglinton Avenue East, Suite 700, Toronto, Ontario M4P 2Y3, Canada
(a division of Pearson Penguin Canada Inc.)
Penguin Books Ltd., 80 Strand, London WC2R 0RL, England
Penguin Group Ireland, 25 St. Stephen's Green, Dublin 2, Ireland (a division of Penguin Books Ltd.)
Penguin Group (Australia), 250 Camberwell Road, Camberwell, Victoria 3124, Australia
(a division of Pearson Australia Group Pty. Ltd.)
Penguin Books India Pvt. Ltd., 11 Community Centre, Panchsheel Park, New Delhi—110 017, India
Penguin Group (NZ), 67 Apollo Drive, Rosedale, North Shore 0632, New Zealand
(a division of Pearson New Zealand Ltd.)
Penguin Books (South Africa) (Pty.) Ltd., 24 Sturdee Avenue, Rosebank, Johannesburg 2196,
South Africa

Penguin Books Ltd., Registered Offices: 80 Strand, London WC2R 0RL, England

This is a work of fiction. Names, characters, places, and incidents either are the product of the author's imagination or are used fictitiously, and any resemblance to actual persons, living or dead, business establishments, events, or locales is entirely coincidental. The publisher does not have any control over and does not assume any responsibility for author or third-party websites or their content.

NUTCASE

A Jove Book / published by arrangement with the author

PRINTING HISTORY
Jove mass-market edition / March 2009

Copyright © 2009 by Charlotte Hughes.
Excerpt from *Hanging by a Thread* copyright © 2009 by Charlotte Hughes.
Cover design by Rita Frangie.
Text design by Laura K. Corless.

All rights reserved.
No part of this book may be reproduced, scanned, or distributed in any printed or electronic form without permission. Please do not participate in or encourage piracy of copyrighted materials in violation of the author's rights. Purchase only authorized editions.
For information, address: The Berkley Publishing Group,
a division of Penguin Group (USA) Inc.,
375 Hudson Street, New York, New York 10014.

ISBN: 978-0-515-14593-9

JOVE®
Jove Books are published by The Berkley Publishing Group,
a division of Penguin Group (USA) Inc.,
375 Hudson Street, New York, New York 10014.
JOVE® is a registered trademark of Penguin Group (USA) Inc.
The "J" design is a trademark of Penguin Group (USA) Inc.

PRINTED IN THE UNITED STATES OF AMERICA

10 9 8 7 6 5 4 3 2 1

If you purchased this book without a cover, you should be aware that this book is stolen property. It was reported as "unsold and destroyed" to the publisher, and neither the author nor the publisher has received any payment for this "stripped book."

To firefighters everywhere,
who risk their lives to serve and protect.
And to their families,
who stand behind them,
despite many sleepless nights.

acknowledgments

Many thanks to the following people:

Marketing genius and webmaster Tara Green of Siren Projects, who worked tirelessly on my behalf and gave me a spectacular website!

Al Zuckerman at Writers House for the strong bond we share. Maya Rock, his assistant, a warm voice on the other end of the line, and a woman who gets things done.

The staff at Berkley, who work behind the scenes to make me look good.

My dear friend and esteemed author Ann B. Ross, who listens to my woes and keeps me laughing with her Miss Julia books.

Janet Evanovich, my personal advisor and friend through thick and thin.

Clinical psychologist Dr. David Berndt, for his continued professional input.

My mother and best friend, Barbara Shelton, for always being there.

And finally, my readers, whose kind words keep me going when I run out of chocolate!

chapter 1

My name is Kate Holly. As a clinical psychologist, I get paid to listen to people's problems. You wouldn't believe some of the stuff I hear. And just when I think I've heard it all, a new patient will come in and blow me out of the water. I'm surprised that my hair hasn't turned white, like when Moses went up to the mountain where God appeared to him as a burning bush.

My colleagues and I often joke that we're even more screwed up than our patients and should all be fitted for straitjackets. We might be on to something. For example, I'm obsessive-compulsive. When I'm stressed, I count things. I do multiplication tables in my head. I prefer even numbers because they are divisible by two. Odd numbers are complicated.

Sort of like my life.

That explains why my ex-husband and I were presently sitting in a marriage counselor's office.

Jay Rush is, and always will be, the love of my life, but we have issues, which only adds to the complexities. Nevertheless, I had tried to postpone our divorce two months ago, only hours before my attorney was to appear in court on my behalf. Unfortunately I'd gotten sidetracked by a wacko patient, and I'd ended up in the ER. That I survived was a miracle, but it proved that I needed to make some serious changes in my life.

Evelyn Hunt was supposed to be the best couple's therapist in town, if not the most expensive. Thankfully, Jay was covering the cost.

As with most high-end psychologists, her so-called hour only lasted forty-five minutes. It was pretty obvious that her clients paid their bills regularly—unlike most of mine—because Evelyn's office looked like the showroom floor at Ethan Allen. She wasted no time getting down to business.

"How's the sex?" she asked me.

The question took me by surprise. I had done my share of marriage counseling and had posed that same question to troubled couples. But this was the first time someone had asked me.

"Fantastic," I said. "Couldn't be better."

Evelyn regarded Jay.

"It's pretty good," he said.

My smile drooped. On a scale of one to ten, his level of enthusiasm rated about a three. I knew he was reluctant to discuss our personal problems with a stranger, even a professional. Most men are like that. In the end, though, he'd agreed we needed help.

"Just pretty good?" I blurted.

He shifted in his chair. The blue nylon jacket he wore matched his eyes. He'd shoved the sleeves to his elbows, exposing arms that were brown and tightly muscled. He worked hard to stay in shape, and it showed. That, combined with his thick dark hair and olive complexion, had turned more heads than mine.

He looked at me. "Sometimes I feel you use sex so we don't have to face our problems."

"That's not true!" I said. Okay, maybe it *was* true, I admitted to myself. But after listening to people's woes all day, the last thing I wanted to do was talk about ours. Or face the fact that we might never work them out.

"Sometimes I feel—" Jay paused. "Like you're holding back," he said. "Like part of you is cut off from me emotionally."

I gave a sigh. When had the man gone all touchy-feely on me? "How can you say that?"

"That's how I feel, Katie. If you don't want to hear the truth, then you shouldn't have asked me to come here."

"Did you want to be here today?" Evelyn asked him.

"Not particularly."

She didn't appear surprised. "But you came anyway," she said. "Why?"

He shrugged. "I suppose I should do my part to try and make our marriage work."

3

Of course, technically we were no longer married, but why quibble over details?

"Do you want your marriage to work?" she asked him.

"Of course I do."

"Have you told Kate that you sometimes feel she is shutting you out?"

"Not in so many words. Like I said, we usually end up in bed."

I sank low in my chair. Evelyn had probably labeled me a sex addict. I wanted to crawl beneath the expensive Persian rug on the floor.

She turned from Jay to me. "Do you think you hold back emotionally?" she asked.

"I'm open to him," I said, flinching at the whiny sound coming out of my mouth. I made that same sound when my mother accused me of not visiting enough. "I share," I added. But it wasn't altogether true. And Jay and I *had* spent a lot of time in the sack during the first month of our attempt at reconciliation. It was the reason we'd made reservations at our favorite restaurants and never showed, missed two films we'd wanted to see, and lost money on concert tickets Jay had purchased.

The room went silent. Evelyn seemed to be waiting for me to fill it. "Okay," I finally said. "I *have* been holding back a little, but that's because Jay has been so critical. He seems to look for reasons to point out my shortcomings with regard to my work."

"Tell Evelyn *why* I criticize you," Jay said.

We locked gazes. "You're just trying to make me look bad," I said.

Jay turned his attention to Evelyn. "Two months ago, Kate was almost strangled by the boyfriend of one of her patients."

"Oh my!" she said.

"That's the first time anything like that ever happened," I said.

Jay went on. "The next day, she blew up her office with a vial of nitroglycerin."

Evelyn gasped.

"He's exaggerating," I said quickly, knowing I'd lost all credibility as a wife *and* a therapist. "There was a small explosion, but it just broke a window and put a little hole in the wall of my reception room. It was an accident."

"An accident?" Jay said. "Was it also an accident that one of your patients tried to run you over in the parking lot two months ago, and you ended up in the ER with a broken wrist?"

Evelyn's mouth formed an O.

"My patient did *not* try to run me over," I said, my irritation growing with Jay's every word. "I was chasing him across the parking lot and I tripped."

Jay gave a grunt. "How many near-death experiences does it take before you realize you might be in the wrong business?"

That pissed me off. "I resent that!" I said, a bit louder

5

than I'd meant to. "I happen to be very good at what I do. Besides, who are *you* to talk about taking risks? *You're* the one who races into burning buildings as everyone else is running out."

He immediately became defensive. "I'm a fire-fighter. That's what I do."

"And I treat people with emotional problems."

"You treat people who need to be locked away," he said. "It's like you're on a mission to find the craziest and most dangerous patients in the world. The sicker the better," he added.

Evelyn's head swiveled from Jay to me and back to Jay. She reminded me of the toy dogs with the bobbing heads that people put in the back of their cars. "See what I mean?" I told her. "To hear him talk you'd think all of my patients were criminally insane when most of them are actually very boring."

"Okay," Evelyn said. "What I'm hearing is that each of you fears for the other's safety because of your occupations, and that it causes discord in your relationship."

Jay nodded.

I nodded.

"It's harder on Kate," Jay said, his tone softening for the first time since we'd entered the room. "Her father was a firefighter who died in the line of duty when she was ten years old."

"I'm so sorry," Evelyn said to me.

"Thank you," I replied, even though I had no desire to dredge up my past.

"I try to take it into consideration," Jay said, "but

6

she's still afraid. She obsesses about every little thing that might go wrong."

"I think I handled it pretty well until you were injured," I said.

He shook his head. "You know that's not true. You questioned me constantly even before the accident. If I told you the truth, you fretted and begged me to quit the department. If I held back information, you accused me of being dishonest. It was one argument after another."

I looked down at my shoes. As much as I wanted to deny it, Jay was telling the truth. The constant bickering had driven a wedge between us, and we'd stopped talking. We'd even stopped having sex. His injury almost eight months ago had been the last straw for me, which is why I'd packed my bags and left.

"Kate knew what I did for a living before we married," Jay said.

I was not surprised by the comment. It always came down to that. My fault. "I thought I could handle it. I'm not the only wife who has fears. Why do you think the divorce rate is so high among firefighters?"

I was rewarded with a dark frown. "So why the hell did you marry me?" he asked.

"Because I fell in love with you, you idiot!" I came close to yelling.

"Time out!" Evelyn said, slicing the air with her arms like a referee. "We need to take a deep breath and calm down."

"I have to get back to the station," Jay said, standing. "This is going nowhere."

"You can't just walk out of marriage counseling!" I said.

"Don't you get it, Katie?" he asked. "I'm tired of arguing about my job and now about your job."

"What are you saying?"

"I'm saying—" He paused. "I've got a lot going on at work right now. This just isn't a good time for me. I'm sorry." He opened the door and quietly let himself out.

My heart sank to my toes.

Evelyn was quiet for a moment. "Are you okay?" she asked finally.

I nodded, but I wasn't okay. What could be more important to Jay than our relationship? "I'll be fine," I said.

I could tell as she reached for her appointment book that she didn't believe me. "Why don't we go ahead and set something up for next Monday. If you need to cancel, just give me twenty-four hours' notice."

I nodded, because I didn't trust my voice.

I found myself anxiously counting traffic lights on the drive to my office. I tried not to think about the possibility of life without Jay. He was not only my lover but my best friend, and one of the most grounded people I knew. After being raised by two women who were the *least* grounded people I knew, I needed a sense of normalcy. And Jay had, despite my objections to his job, provided it.

My mother and aunt were partially responsible for

my neuroses. Picture two plus-sized women, identical twins, in their midfifties, with big platinum hair and inch-long eyelashes. Even before I'd lost my father, they'd been hard-core junk dealers, which meant I'd been raised in a house surrounded by more crap than on *Sanford and Son*. Our living room made Graceland look like something out of *Southern Living*. They referred to themselves as the Junk Sisters. In school, I was known as the daughter of a Junk Sister. I'm fairly certain that's why nobody asked me to the senior prom.

Red was their signature color. They wore red overalls and rode around in a candy apple red six-ton 2007 Navistar CLT pickup truck, which they'd purchased once their business had taken off and become a huge success. It was twenty-one feet long and capable of hauling more junk than Amtrak. Before they had arrived, as my mother liked to say, selling junk had been a hobby of sorts. My earliest memories were of me digging through the trash in ritzy neighborhoods on garbage day while they kept watch from my father's battered truck, the engine running so we could make a quick getaway if need be. I'd been coaxed inside every Dumpster within a fifty-mile radius of Atlanta, and I knew everybody's name at the local flea market where we rented a booth on weekends.

They had become very successful over the years, having turned their junk into sculptures, wall art, and painted furniture. Their new studio in Little Five Points drew high-end interior decorators and wealthy customers. The sign outside their store read "Junque" because my mother thought it sounded sophisticated. They made a killing.

While I was enormously proud of my mother, she and I bumped heads constantly. She often stuck her nose in my business, and she had more advice than a self-help book, even though, at thirty-two, I had read most of them. She was bossy and overbearing and could induce guilt in the best of us. I recalled her doing the same to my father. Sometimes, when I was at the end of my rope with her, I couldn't help but wonder if he'd chosen to stay in that burning building.

I pulled into the parking lot next to my office and was suddenly overcome with a choking sense of dread. I had been served an eviction notice two months ago, a result of the aforementioned explosion. I'd spent the first month begging my landlord to reconsider. He'd agreed to give me an extra month, during which time I'd searched high and low for affordable office space. The only place that had come close was in a one-story building that housed a cab company and a lending operation called Snappy Cash, owned and operated by a seedy man named Freddie who wore white shoes and polyester slacks and had a terrible comb-over. It would have meant sharing a bathroom and kitchen space with people who appeared hygienically challenged and who were not overly concerned that one or two of their front teeth were missing.

I now had until five p.m. on Friday to find a new

place, at which time my landlord planned to change the locks on my doors.

I spoke to several of the people who got on and off the elevator as I rode to my office on the fourth floor. I knew most of them since my best friend, receptionist, and self-appointed PR person, Mona Epps, held an open house on the first Monday of every month in hopes of building my practice. It was a catered event where she passed out brochures on mental health issues and saw that everyone left with my business card. Since she was rich and paid for it all, there was little I could do about it.

The events hadn't drawn many patients, but Mona and I were well liked by the other tenants.

I heard loud singing before I opened the door leading into my reception room. Inside, I found a striking but disheveled woman in a sequined cowgirl outfit and ten-gallon hat, belting out the words to an old country song, "Help Me Make It Through the Night." The fact that I wasn't *surprised* to find a complete stranger performing a nightclub act in my office said a lot about what I faced on a daily basis.

Sitting at her desk, Mona gave me an eye roll. I simply stood there quietly while the woman sang, using a hairbrush as her microphone. Finally, she finished. I smiled and clapped and Mona did likewise. I'm sure we were in silent agreement that the woman would never see her name in lights.

"Who are you?" she asked me.

I noted a slight odor coming from her; like maybe she needed a hot shower and a bar of deodorant soap. "I'm Dr. Kate Holly," I said. "You can call me Kate." I smiled. "And you are?"

The woman looked surprised. "You don't recognize me?" She pulled off her cowboy hat, and I almost winced at the sight of her hair, dyed coal black and chopped in an unflattering style.

Mona cleared her voice and gave me the special look we shared when weird people showed up in my office, which was often. "Kate, meet Marie Osmond," she said. "I didn't recognize her at first either. She looks much younger in person."

The Marie Osmond wannabe smiled.

She looked vaguely familiar, but I couldn't place her. The only thing I knew for certain was that she couldn't possibly be Marie Osmond, whom I'd recently seen on *Dancing with the Stars*.

"I'm honored," I said, taking her hand and shaking it. I noticed her nails were dirty and chipped. There were bruises on her arms.

"Miss Osmond is reinventing herself," Mona said. "She plans to take the country music industry by storm. And you'll never guess what else. She has walked away from all her fame and fortune and started from scratch."

Marie nodded. "That's right. I gave it all up—" She paused and snapped her fingers. "Just like that. A real country western star sings about hardship, broken hearts, and old pickup trucks," she added. "They don't sing songs about shopping on Rodeo Drive."

Mona gave me another of our special looks. "Marie has been looking for gigs in Atlanta, but she hasn't had much luck."

The woman gave a huff. "It has nothing to do with talent, of course. People would hire me in a second if I would agree to sing the old Donny and Marie songs." She gave a massive sigh. "I swear, if I have to hear 'Puppy Love' again, I'll barf up my spleen. Anyway, last night I auditioned for this guy named Rusty who owns Rusty's Place, and he gave me your address and phone number and said you had a lot of connections."

I blinked several times. It was a lot to take in at once, and the woman spoke at warp speed. I knew Rusty well. Jay and I often ate at his restaurant because he had the best steaks in town. Obviously, Rusty had decided the woman had serious problems and sent her my way.

"I had doubts about coming to see you," Marie said. "I mean, I grew up in the music industry, and there's nothing I don't already know about the business, but as I was pulling into your parking lot I saw your phone number written in the sky with the words 'Compassionate Friend.' I knew it was a sign from God that I was supposed to be here."

I nodded. Most psychologists, upon hearing about signs from God, would immediately suspect they were dealing with a psychotic or a Jehovah's Witness. Not true in my case. Mona had hired a pilot to pull a banner over the city of Atlanta advertising my services, hoping one day I would be famous and have my own talk show.

"Well, I'll certainly do my best to help," I said after a moment, "but I don't know anything about the entertainment industry. I'm a clinical psychologist."

Marie glanced from me to Mona and then back at me. I could tell she was unsettled and probably very confused. "You're a shrink?" she said. "Why would Rusty send me to a shrink?"

I tried to think of a good response.

"Maybe he thought we could give you the name of a good hair stylist," Mona said.

I floundered for a reply. "Well, trying to reinvent yourself can be very stressful," I began, "and to be perfectly honest, you look worn out." Actually, she looked like hell.

"Don't you *get it*?" Marie asked Mona. "I'm supposed to look like this. I'm trying to appeal to those who struggle every month to make payments on their mobile homes. I want to reach out to the person who has no one in his life to love except a Bluetick hound dog. I'm singing to the broken masses."

"Oh, that just gave me goose pimples," Mona said, rubbing her arms.

Marie shrugged. "Besides, I've been sleeping in my car."

"That's awfully dangerous," I said. It probably explained why she needed a shower.

"Oh, I could stay in the fanciest hotel in town if I wanted, but that would not be true to my new image. Everything I own is in the trunk of my car, including a dozen country western outfits. You'd flip if I told you how much money I spent on them."

I had by now realized that I was most likely dealing with a woman with bipolar disorder. "Marie, when was the last time you slept?" I asked.

She looked at me as though I were speaking a foreign language. "What day is this?"

"Monday."

"Oh, I'm sure I must've slept over the weekend, but I was mostly looking for gigs."

"How did you get those bruises?" I asked, motioning to her arms.

She avoided eye contact. "I don't remember."

"Why don't we talk in my office," I said, feeling the need to sit down and take a deep breath. The woman was exhausting.

"I don't have much time," Marie said. "I need a list of your contacts so I can get moving."

I did not think she would be safe on her own. "First, you need a solid business plan," I said. "And you need to write out your short- and long-term goals. A clear plan will save you a lot of time, and it will assist me in helping you."

She seemed to ponder it. "That makes sense. Now I know why Rusty sent me to you."

I led her inside my office and invited her to sit. I grabbed a fresh legal pad and two pens from my coffee mug so that I would still have an even number left inside. I handed them to her. My plan was to keep her occupied until I could make arrangements to get her help, which, in her case, probably meant hospitalization. I'd seen enough manic highs in my life to recognize the symptoms. The flip side of mania is depression. I needed to make certain that Marie wasn't sleeping in her car when she hit the emotional skids.

"Perhaps you'd like to list the reasons you've decided to reinvent yourself in the first place," I said.

She nodded enthusiastically. "What an excellent idea!"

I opened my desk drawer and pulled out a release form that would give me a legal right to share information related to Marie. "I would like to be able to discuss your situation with a friend and colleague of mine," I said. "He and I sometimes work together on cases. I trust his opinion."

"No problem." She signed the paper and handed it back to me. She was scribbling furiously on the legal pad as I left the room.

Mona was filing her nails. "That woman is off her rocker," she said without looking up.

"Would you get Thad Glazer on the line? Try his cell phone first."

"Uh-oh," Mona said. "You know what happens every time you ask him for a favor."

Dr. Thad Glazer was my ex-boyfriend, and the center of his own universe. He was also a psychiatrist to the wealthy, meaning he never worried about his

patients' checks bouncing. I'd broken it off with Thad
some four and a half years ago when I caught him
cheating. I'd later met and married Jay. Thad still be-
lieved I did it to get back at him. Now that I was officially divorced, he thought we should pick up where
we'd left off. I did not share his opinion. But, despite it
all, I could pretty much count on him to see my patients for medication therapy. In return, I took on his
more troublesome patients for talk therapy, which is
how I'd ended up with the major nutcases.

I was hoping Thad could get the commitment order
drawn up more quickly than I could and, hopefully,
find a spare bed in the psychiatric ward at the hospital
we often used. He had a silver tongue that came in
handy during crunch time.

Mona dialed Thad's number and waited. "Hello,
Thad," Mona said. "Kate needs to speak with you.
There's some wacko here who thinks she's Marie Osmond. I think Kate wants to throw her in the loony
bin." Mona held her hand over the receiver. "Thad
wants to know if you're naked."

I didn't bother with a response. In my line of work,
there are certain ethical standards we are supposed to
follow. Mona and Thad ignored them. But firing Mona
was out of the question. Not only was she my best
friend, she worked for free.

I held out my hand and Mona gave me the phone.
"Thad, I've got a bipolar woman in my office who
needs to be admitted to the hospital. She's also going
to require meds. Lots of meds," I added.

Thad chuckled. "That sort of places you in the predicament of needing me," he said.

"Yeah, okay." It was easier to play along.

"Say the words, Kate."

"I need you, Thad."

Mona shook her head sadly.

"I'll have to reschedule my tennis match," he said. "I wish you'd called me yesterday when I had more time on my hands."

I tried to sound sympathetic. "I'm sorry you'll be forced to spend the afternoon practicing psychiatry instead of your backhand," I said.

"You're not sorry. Which brings me to the next question," he said. "What's in it for me?"

I'd been subconsciously waiting for Thad to say something inappropriate, because that's what he usually did. He pushed my buttons, yanked my chain, and all of the above. As a professional, I knew I should try to rise above it. I seldom did.

"You owe me, Thad. Does the name George Moss mean anything to you?" George was the patient who'd carried into my office the vial of nitroglycerin that had ultimately led to the explosion. Thad had referred him to me.

"That was not my fault," Thad said. "You are the one who lost your temper and threw the vial against the wall and blew up your own office."

"Maybe so, but you're the one who told me George Moss was harmless and that the vial contained his insulin. You should have had it checked by a lab before sending him to my office. After all, he threatened to blow up your place as well."

"He was histrionic, Kate. That's what histrionics do. Why didn't *you* have the vial checked out?"

Thad had a point. The truth was George had created such a frenzy of drama for himself and others that nobody, myself included, had taken him seriously.

"You can't hold that over my head for the rest of my life," Thad said.

"Yes, I can. It's more fun that way. Now, the patient we'll be consulting on goes by the name of Marie Osmond."

"Why?"

"Because that's who she thinks she is," I said. "Personally, I would have chosen to be Celine Dion, but that's just me."

"Are we talking voluntary commitment here?" he asked.

"I wouldn't count on it."

He sighed. "Okay, I'll get on it right away and have the hospital send an ambulance for her. Since my day is shot anyway, I can probably meet you over there in a couple of hours."

"Thank you, Thad," I said, meaning it.

"And, hey, we can go to dinner later and discuss our findings. It'll give us a chance to talk about us."

"There *is* no us, Thad."

"Kate, Kate, Kate. I know you've been through a rough time, but you have to move on. I could help you forget Jay Rush ever existed."

19

I knew Thad's remedy for everything from stress to ingrown toenails was a pitcher of margaritas and a stint in his hot tub followed by all-night sex. But the only thing likely to make me forget Jay was a full frontal lobotomy.

"I have to go, Thad," I said. "I'll see you at the hospital." I hung up and handed the phone to Mona.

"Did he try to talk you into having phone sex?" she asked.

"Not this time."

chapter 2

....

Marie was still writing out her business plan when
my next patient, Eddie Franks, arrived. He'd spent a
few years in prison for swindling several old ladies out
of their retirement. Since he'd invested a large portion
of the money in the stock market, he had been able to
make restitution, as ordered by the court; thus serving
less time behind bars. Of course, Eddie, being the con
he was, had tried to convince the judge he was simply
trying to build the nice ladies' savings. But the fact
that he had tried—and failed—to cover his sly finan-
cial tracks by using an alias had "guilty" written all
over him. The judge had thrown him in the slammer.
Weekly therapy sessions were one of the conditions of
Eddie's parole.

In his late fifties, he was still handsome, impeccably dressed, and one of the smoothest-talking men I'd

ever met. Except for Jay, who could charm a woman right out of her undies. But I didn't want to think about Jay or what it was like to feel his mouth on me and his warm flesh against mine, since I had no idea where our relationship was headed.

I decided it was best not to disturb Marie by going into my office for Eddie's file. I grabbed a legal tablet and pen from the supply room so that I could take notes. I pulled Mona aside. "Don't let Marie leave this office," I whispered to her.

"I'm on it," Mona said.

I asked Eddie to follow me down the hall to my small kitchenette. I motioned for him to sit at the table, and I joined him. "I have a situation on my hands this morning," I said, "so we'll have to talk in here. We may be interrupted." I had no idea how long it would take Thad to get commitment papers on Marie because each case was different.

Eddie shrugged as if it were no big deal. "Just as long as you tell my parole officer I was here," he said and smiled. His teeth were too perfect to be his own, but he still had a full head of salt-and-pepper hair, more salt than pepper.

"How was your week?" I asked quickly. Despite jail time, Eddie had been able to find a job in a prestigious menswear store and had made top salesman within the first couple of weeks.

"You're looking at the new manager of the most elite menswear store in town," he announced proudly.

I was impressed. "Congratulations!"

"I plan to have my own store one day."

"Slow down, Eddie," I said, although it was easy to get caught up in his enthusiasm. He was the kind of person people flocked to at a party. "You need to take it one day at a time and follow through with the conditions of your parole." I did not want Eddie to backslide into his old habits.

"I can't help being impatient," he said. "I spent three years of my life behind bars."

I nodded. I liked Eddie, but it bothered me that he was more focused on how his crimes had affected *him*. He spent very little time thinking about the women he'd cheated. I wanted to hear remorse. I wanted Eddie to be genuinely sorry for what he'd done.

Our session had just ended when Mona appeared in the doorway. "Your mom and aunt are here. They decided to surprise you and invite you to join them for an early lunch."

"Did you tell them I had an emergency?"

"Like it would make a difference?" Mona said. "Oh, and Thad called. He's still working on that little task you gave him."

"I'm going to have to do something nice for him," I said.

Mona crossed her eyes. It was a technique she had perfected since coming to work for me. "I'm sure he'll come up with something."

The three of us made our way to the reception area, where I found my mother and aunt thumbing through old magazines. It would have been hard to miss the

Junk Sisters. My grandmother had chosen to name them Dixie and Trixie. "Good morning," I said.

My mother looked at me. "You're too thin." She turned to my aunt Trixie. "Doesn't Kate look thin?"

"I think she looks great," my aunt said.

My aunt was the peacemaker and spent much of her time trying to smooth out the misunderstandings between my mother and me.

My mother looked annoyed. "How can you say Kate looks great when she's practically skin and bones?" She turned to me. "Are you sick?"

I debated telling her that I had mad cow disease. "I'm fine," I said instead. I couldn't really blame her for being concerned about my weight, though. My separation and divorce had whittled me from a size ten to a six. Mona's housekeeper, Mrs. Perez, had altered a lot of my clothes since I couldn't afford to buy a new wardrobe.

"We're here to take you to lunch," Aunt Trixie said, changing the subject.

My mother nodded. "You'll have to hurry, on account of we're double-parked."

I envisioned her monster pickup truck piled high with junk, blocking half the cars in the parking lot. "I'm sorry, but I can't go," I said. "I've got an emergency." I noted Eddie eyeing them curiously, but I wasn't surprised. People on the street often stopped and stared at them, too.

"How can you have an emergency?" my mother asked. "You're not a real doctor."

"That's not a very nice thing to say," Aunt Trixie told her.

"We've got a serious nutcase in the next room waiting to be transferred to the asylum," Mona said. "Kate is under a lot of stress right now."

I knew Mona was trying to help, so I didn't bother to remind her that we didn't refer to our patients as nutcases or that psychiatric wards were not called asylums.

My mother stepped closer. "I don't know how you work with these crazies," she whispered. "No wonder you're so thin and depressed. I read in yesterday's paper that the FDA just approved an antidepressant that was guaranteed not to interfere with your sex life. You should look into it."

"I'm not depressed, Mom," I whispered back. "Maybe we could have lunch another time."

"Trixie and I could be dead and buried by the time you worked us into your schedule," she said. "How would that make you feel?"

"I would feel terribly guilty," I said and saw the look of satisfaction on her face. She had succeeded in doing her job for the day.

Eddie stepped forward. "Ladies, why don't you allow me to escort you to lunch in Dr. Holly's stead?"

I opened my mouth in protest, then closed it. I couldn't warn my mom and aunt that Eddie was a shyster and an ex-con without losing my license.

"Who are you?" my mother blurted out.

"Edward Franks, at your service." He gave a slight

bow. "I'm a close, um, acquaintance of your daughter, and I would consider it an honor to take the two of you to lunch. It'll be my treat."

"Don't you have to get back to work?" I asked Eddie hopefully.

"I have plenty of time," he assured me, his tone as smooth and sugary as maple syrup.

Mona shot me a look. Since Eddie had confided in her, it was obvious she didn't like the idea of him being alone with my mother and aunt any more than I did.

"I suppose it'll be okay," my mother finally said. My aunt nodded in agreement.

Eddie opened the door and motioned them through with a flourish while Mona and I watched, open-mouthed. Eddie gave me a hearty wink and followed them out.

Mona shook her head. "At least I'll be able to say I was there when it happened," she said.

I looked at her. "What do you mean?"

"I'll be able to say I was present the day your inheritance walked out the door."

I was still waiting to hear from Thad when my next patient arrived. I had checked on Marie and found she'd already burned through half the pages in the tablet. I'd scanned several pages, noting that most of what she'd written lacked coherency; then, I asked Mona to fax them and the signed release form to Thad. It would give him a better idea of what we were dealing with.

I led Arnie Decker to my makeshift office in the kitchenette and invited him to sit. Arnie was a retired marine turned executive chef who claimed he'd been trapped in a woman's body for as long as he could remember. It was a case of gender identity disorder. In stark contrast to his broad shoulders and a large tattoo of an eagle on one bulging bicep, he was dressed in short shorts and a glittery tee that exposed his pierced navel. Ten painted toenails peeked out from the tops of his beaded sandals.

"How was your week?" I asked, flipping to a new page in my legal pad.

Arnie gave a massive sigh. "I've decided to tell my family the truth about my, um, gender issues. I'm tired of the lies and deceit. I'm tired of trying to be the person my old man expects me to be. I need to live my life the way I want."

I could sort of relate. When I told my mother I wanted to become a psychologist, she had taken me out to the double garage and showed me her world of junk. "This could all be yours one day," she'd said, as though we were gazing down from the heavens at the entire universe and all its riches. "Why would you turn your back on the family business to become a shrink?" she'd asked.

Arnie sighed again.

"How do you think your father will take the news?" I asked.

"It won't be good. But in all fairness, I need to warn him of what's to come."

Arnie had decided to pursue gender reassignment surgery. Together, we had researched it carefully, and I had spoken to a couple of professionals. Surgical reassignment was available only for extreme cases of GID. That Arnie had been unable to maintain normal male-female relationships, and had considered suicide more than once because he was so miserable, made him a candidate in my mind.

Easier said than done. Arnie would have to jump through a number of hoops in order to meet the criteria. He would need to spend months in therapy and actually live and dress like a woman before a doctor would agree to start him on a regimen of hormonal injections that would begin to bring about the changes he desired.

"I've decided to change my name to Arnell," he said. "Once I tell my father the truth, I plan to start living as a woman full-time." He clasped his hands together and leaned forward. "Dr. Holly, I want you to be with me when I tell him."

My stomach flipped and flopped like a fish pulled from the water. Arnie's father was a hard-core retired marine who'd gone off the deep end when he found a rag doll in his son's room. Arnie had been eleven years old at the time. His father had been trying to turn him into a man's man ever since. Not only did I not want to be in the same room when Arnie told his father the truth, I didn't want to be on the same planet.

"Wouldn't your father feel uncomfortable having an outsider present?" I asked hopefully.

・ Nutcase ・

"I can't do it alone," he said. "I'm going to need support. Now that I've made my decision, I'd like to get it over with. When is the soonest I can get another appointment?"

I hesitated. I wasn't going to have an office after Friday, so it would have to be soon. I checked my appointment book. "How does Wednesday afternoon sound?" I was already dreading it. I wondered if he would fall for my mad cow disease story.

The ambulance arrived for Marie, accompanied by a police officer, as I was escorting Arnie out. "I'll need a few minutes to talk to the patient," I said.

I found Marie sitting on the sofa, flexing her right hand. She looked at me. "I have writer's cramp."

I took the chair beside her. "Marie, I know how important your country western music career is, but I think you need to put it on the back burner for now."

She looked alarmed. "I can't! My fans will forget about me."

I touched her shoulder in hopes of calming her. "You've neglected your health," I said. "You can't remember when you last slept, and I'll bet you haven't eaten a decent meal in days. You're in no condition to think about a new career." I paused, knowing she was not going to like what I had to say. "I want you to go into the hospital for a few days."

"You can't be serious!" she said. "What will I tell my fans? What will I tell the press?"

29

"We'll try to keep it quiet, but if anyone should find out, we'll say you're suffering from exhaustion."

Her eyes suddenly hardened. "I should have known something like this would happen. You're jealous. It irks the hell out of you that I have all this talent and you have none. You don't want to see me succeed."

"I want to see you healthy," I said.

She threw the legal pad on the floor. "Do I have a choice in the matter?" she asked. "Or do they plan to drag me to the psych ward and drug me?" She met my surprised gaze. "This ain't my first rodeo, lady."

"Then I think it's especially important that we try to cooperate with each other the best we can. There are EMTs out front waiting to take you to the hospital."

"What if I refuse to go? Then what?" she added.

I sat back in my chair and regarded her. "I think you know the answer to that," I said. "You'll crash and burn, and there will be nobody to help you."

She sat there quietly for a moment, but I could see the anger burning in her eyes. "If they try to cuff me, I'll kick and scream and bite."

"I'll ask them not to, but you'll have to cooperate." We both stood and headed for the door. I opened it and stepped outside with Marie on my heels. "Miss Osmond is ready to go," I said. "She doesn't need to be restrained."

Mona and I were quiet as Marie was led out. The police officer nodded at me before he closed the door behind him.

"Boy, am I glad I don't have *your* job," Mona said. "I used to think it would be cool helping people, but it must be awful hearing about other people's problems day in and day out. I would hate to be you."

The door opened, and two teenage girls in slut-wear walked through, followed by their parents, who hoped family counseling would put an end to the hostility that was wrecking their home. It never failed; each session turned into a yelling match. Maybe Mona was right; being me was no picnic.

Thad and the head nurse of the psychiatric unit, Edith Wright, were waiting for me in a conference room when I arrived at the hospital. Edith was a large woman with reddish orange hair and a multitude of freckles. She'd spent twenty-five years in the psychiatric ward, and she was tough as beef jerky. She was also the only female who didn't have a crush on Thad.

"Sorry I'm late," I said quickly, sitting in a chair across the table from Thad and noting that Edith had chosen to position herself at the head. She obviously wanted to make it clear she was in charge.

"I've already met with Marie Osmond," Thad said, "and she told me how you are out to ruin her country music career. Frankly, Kate, I'm shocked that you would step all over someone's hopes and dreams."

"I'm envious of her talent."

Edith gave a grunt. "I've heard her sing. She's no Reba McEntire."

31

"I think we should let Thad break the news to her," I told Edith.

He leaned back in his chair and smiled the smile that had captured a thousand hearts. Thad was an enigma. As always, he was immaculately dressed in a custom tailored suit of Italian silk, and he looked more like the CEO of a Fortune 500 company than a psychiatrist. Oddly enough, between golf games and tennis matches, Thad was damn good at what he did.

"So, what do you think?" I asked him. "Have you got a diagnosis?"

"She's screwed up," he said.

"I'll bet you got that straight out of the *Diagnostic and Statistical Manual*."

"Yep. Good thing this hotel has locks on the doors."

"Very funny," I said.

Thad looked at Edith. "Kate used to be a barrel of laughs when we were lovers," he said. "She had a great sense of humor."

"Thanks for sharing, Thad," I said.

Edith gave him a withering look. "Gee, Dr. Glazer, as much as I would love to hear the minute details of your sexual prowess, I do have other patients."

Thad made a *tsk*ing sound. "You're a cold woman, Edith." He turned to me. "Your diagnosis of bipolar disorder was right on. Marie could barely sit still long enough to talk, and she was hyperverbal. She had also just finished writing a song about an old cowboy that she is certain will earn her a Grammy. I think it's safe to say she's exhibiting signs of grandiosity."

"Yeah, I noticed." Grandiose behavior was common in bipolar patients.

"I've already ordered blood work, a thyroid profile, and an EKG," he said. "I'm going to start her on Vistaril and a new mood stabilizer that's getting rave reviews. Supposedly, it kicks in much faster than the others." He grinned. "I also had Edith inject a sedative so the staff doesn't have to chase Marie all over the unit. Which is why Edith is being so nice to me today," he added, giving her a hearty wink.

Edith yawned.

"Anything else?" I asked.

"Marie didn't even try to flirt with me."

Sometimes it was best to ignore Thad's comments. This was one of those times. "Do we have anything like a patient history on Marie, or is that too much to hope for?"

Edith picked up a file and opened it. "I did the intake. She gave me zip. I take it you noticed the bruises. She refuses to talk about them."

"She claims she doesn't remember how she got them," I said. I looked from Edith to Thad. "If that's it, I should probably look in on her."

"If you wake her I'll take you out," Edith said.

Thad slid his gaze from her to me. "She means it. I hear she carries a loaded weapon in her purse."

"I don't need a gun," Edith said. "I have my bare hands."

"I'll come back another time," I said quickly.

Thad and I thanked her. She buzzed us through the

33

double doors, and we headed for the elevators. "I think Edith is hot for me," he said, punching the button to call the elevator.

"She's doing a really good job of hiding it, don't you think?" After several seconds, I stabbed the button for the elevator. "These things move slower than a drunken mule," I muttered.

He looked at me. "How come you're so irritable? Did somebody steal your favorite feminine deodorant spray? What was the brand you used? Fresh Flowers?"

"Cut it out, Thad." The elevator door opened and we stepped inside. "I have a lot going on in my life right now." I pressed the button to the lobby, and we started down.

"How did your marriage counseling session with Jay go this morning?" I snapped my head around, my surprised gaze meeting his. "Oh hell," he said, covering his eyes with one hand. "Could we forget I just asked you that question?"

"Mona told you?" I felt betrayed.

"It was my fault, Kate. I called the office this morning to ask about Alice Smithers's medication, and Mona started getting all weird on me when I asked where you were. I used my great charm and people skills. She couldn't help herself. Please don't rat me out."

I tried to hide my embarrassment. "I don't have to tell you that marriage counseling takes time," I said. "First sessions are always tense."

"That's why I steer clear of them." He snapped his fingers. "Hey, I know how to cheer you up. How about I spring for lunch and buy you a chili dog? You love the chili dogs here."

"Yeah, but I need to head back to my office."

"What's fifteen minutes out of your day?"

My mouth was already watering. I grinned. "Extra onions?"

He winced. "There goes my idea about renting a room afterward." He pressed the button that would take us to the cafeteria, and soon after we stepped out. "Why don't you grab a table outside," he said. "It won't take me long to go through the line."

I pushed through the glass door leading to the court-yard, where white wrought iron tables and flower beds filled with mums looked inviting. The cool November air felt good after a summer that had reached some all-time high temperature. As they did each year, the local news felt compelled to fry an egg on the sidewalk to prove just how hot it was. I'd been tempted to cook a pot roast on my front walk and prove the annual egg thing lame.

Thad joined me a few minutes later, bearing a tray of chili dogs, salt and vinegar potato chips, and soft drinks. "Just like old times, eh?" he said. "You're the only woman I know who likes salt and vinegar potato chips."

I noted the pile of onions on the chili dogs. "Yum," I said, reaching for one. I took a bite. "Oh man," I said.

"Not bad for hospital food," Thad said. "Reminds

35

me of that little hot dog stand at Emory," he added. "Those were the days."

That's where Thad and I had met. I'd been working on my doctorate at the time. "Sometimes I really miss them," I said.

He took a sip of his drink, set down his cup, and regarded me. "So, where do you and Jay stand, if you don't mind me asking?"

"He wasn't real happy when he left. It's just one more thing to worry about," I added.

"What do you mean?"

"I'm being evicted from my office because of the explosion."

Thad frowned. "That was two months ago."

"I managed to convince my landlord to give me an extension."

"Meaning you did your fake crying act."

"A girl has to do what a girl has to do. I've got until Friday at five p.m. to get out."

"Damn, that's four days from now! Where are you moving?"

"Dunno, Thad. Do you have any idea what it costs to lease a decent office these days?"

He tossed his napkin aside and leaned forward on his elbows. "This is my fault. I wish I'd never referred George Moss to you. I wish neither of us had ever laid eyes on him."

I shrugged. "Hey, like you said, I'm the one who lost my temper and threw the vial of nitroglycerin against the wall. Nobody forced me."

"You would never have done it if you had known Moss was serious. I should have called the police the day he brought it into my office," he said. "I acted irresponsibly, Kate, and I can't apologize enough for getting you involved."

"I'm just thankful he's not my patient anymore," I said. I finished my chili dog.

"What does Jay say about the office?"

"He doesn't know. You're the first person I've told."

Thad looked pleased. "That says a lot, Kate. It shows that you trust me."

"You won me over with the chili dog."

Thad sipped his drink in silence and I polished off my chips and his. "Actually, this couldn't have happened at a better time," he said. "At least for me," he added. "I've been looking for a psychologist to share my office."

I glanced at him. "See, that's the reason I didn't tell Jay or Mona. I don't want a handout. I don't want people feeling I need to be rescued."

"Who said anything about rescuing you?"

"I'm thinking I should apply at the mental health center. The pay isn't so great, but I won't have the overhead. Plus, they have a great insurance plan."

"You tried that, remember? Too many rules and regulations. Besides, I wouldn't have mentioned wanting to bring in a psychologist if I weren't serious."

"Yeah, right." I sucked down the last of my soft drink.

"You know I don't have time for talk therapy. It's all

I can do to keep up with my patients' meds, not to mention trying to stay on top of the latest studies and trials and warnings."

I knew Thad's job was not as easy as I sometimes made it out to be. One drug might prove beneficial to tens of thousands of patients, only to be snatched off the market by the FDA at a moment's notice if a handful of patients suffered adverse reactions. Sometimes it took days or weeks to find the right medication and dosage for a patient.

"I couldn't afford the parking at your place," I said.

"You could if you had a better clientele," he pointed out.

I looked at him. "You're serious?"

"It's the perfect plan. And I'd feel less guilty over George Moss."

I had to smile at the earnest look on his face. "I don't know, Thad. I sort of like making you feel guilty. I must be turning into my mother."

"I'm talking about a business arrangement, Kate. I'd insist on having my attorney draw up a contract. You would agree to see a certain number of my patients for talk therapy to cover part of the rent, and you would still have plenty of time to build your own practice." He paused. "You would be treating people who actually pay their bills."

I must've looked stunned, because he sat back in his chair as though giving me space to think. "You don't have to make up your mind this minute," he said. "You probably will want to pass it by Jay first."

I did not want to discuss Jay with Thad. "I appreciate the offer, Thad," I said, "but I need to find a place
where I can take Mona with me. We're a team."

"There is plenty of room to add another desk in the
reception room," he said. "Mona and Bunny would get
along great."

"Bunny?"

"My new receptionist. She's hot."

"Does Bunny know how to use a computer?"

"She doesn't have to."

I chuckled. "Same old Thad."

"You could change me, you know."

"I'd need a big gun."

He checked his wristwatch. "If I hurry, I can still
get in a little tennis. Would you mind?" He reached for
the tray.

I shooed him away. "Go play tennis," I said. "I'll
clean up."

"Don't forget my offer." He stood, kissed the top of
my head, and hurried off.

I sat there for a moment, trying to gather my thoughts.
I should have told Jay about the eviction. Being evicted
was no small thing, and Jay was still sort of like a husband. I regretted that I'd kept it to myself, because now
it would be even more difficult to tell him. I tried to re-
hearse in my mind how I would break it to him, but I
was interrupted when someone called my name.

I looked up to find an acquaintance, Carter Atkins,
standing beside the table with a tray. "Hello, Carter," I
said. "I haven't seen you in a while."

"Mind if I join you?" he asked.

I knew I had to get going, but I didn't want to appear rude. Carter was an orderly at the hospital, as well as a volunteer fireman. He was in his late thirties and reminded me of the actor John Malkovich. "Have a seat," I said. "I'm sorry, but I only have a few minutes. I have to get back to the office."

He took the chair across from me and began unwrapping his sandwich, eyeing me as he did so. "You're looking good, Kate," he said. "Heard you and Jay got a divorce."

I knew there were no secrets in the fire department, but I was put off by Carter's bluntness. "It happens to the best of us," I said. I smiled, gathered my purse closer, and reached for the tray.

"I know what it's like being alone. Except for having my mother around, of course, but she's in the early stages of Alzheimer's so she fades in and out."

"I'm sorry," I said. "I didn't know." He shrugged. "You've never been married?"

"No. I never found anyone I thought could get along with Mother." He leaned closer. "Guess what? I'm studying for the fireman's exam."

"That's wonderful," I said.

"I figure that with as much time as I spend at the station, I might as well be on the payroll, you know?" He smiled for the first time. "Hey, you should see the new probie."

A probie was the same thing as a new recruit. "What's he like?" I asked.

"He's a she. A real babe," he added, "and don't think she doesn't know it."

"When did she start?"

"Couple of weeks ago. You ask me, she's a pain in the butt."

I couldn't hide my surprise. Jay had not mentioned her.

"We got in a guy from Texas about the same time. He's got a lot of experience compared to the new girl. Did I mention she's stacked?"

I was having mixed reactions to the news. Jay usually shared what went on at the station. I knew most of the guys, as well as the women, by name. It sort of proved how distant he'd become over the past few weeks. I felt bummed out as I checked the time.

"I'm not surprised he forgot to mention it to you," Carter said. "There have been a rash of fires in the past few days that look kind of suspicious."

"Arson?" I asked.

"Looks that way. Same MO. You know what that means."

I nodded. It meant there was a serial arsonist. "Do they have any suspects?"

Carter shook his head. "Whoever is setting the fires knows what he's doing."

My day had just gotten even worse. "I have to get back to the office."

I started to get up, but Carter put his hand on mine. "Listen, you ever need someone to talk to, I'm your guy."

· Charlotte Hughes ·

"Thank you."

"I'm serious. The problem with most people today is they don't take the time to care about others. I'm not that way. I don't like it when people are hurting."

"I'm fine, Carter," I said.

He released my hand, and I said good-bye. I carried the tray to the trash can and dumped the garbage. I glanced Carter's way and found him watching me. I tried to ignore the strange sensation in my stomach as I hurried on.

He sure was an odd bird.

chapter 3

·····························

I arrived at my office with time to spare before my next patient. Mona was on the phone. She didn't look happy. "I can't believe you're canceling another date," she said to the person on the other end.

Obviously, she was talking to her boyfriend, Liam, a medical intern and hunk. Liam was younger than Mona, but he didn't know it because she'd lied about her age. She covered her lie with Botox.

"I have to go," she said. She hung up.

"Problems?" I asked.

"I'm tired of making plans only to have Liam cancel at the last minute. I think he's losing interest."

"I doubt it," I said.

"I think he's got something going with one of those young nurses. They follow him around like puppies."

She sighed. "Let's change the subject. Did you get Psycho Woman admitted to the hospital?"

"She is resting comfortably, thanks to good drugs. I need to schedule a time to see her every day. Maybe at lunch," I said.

Mona checked the appointment book she kept on her desk. "That'll work."

I sat in one of the chairs. "We need to talk," I said. "Actually, I should have had this conversation with you a couple of months ago."

"Is this about the eviction notice?"

"You *know* about that?"

"Everybody in the building knows, and they think it stinks. They started a petition, but your jerk landlord ignored it. He's probably planning to raise the rent for the next occupant."

I felt mortified that word had gotten around to the other tenants. "Why didn't you tell me?" I asked.

"I was waiting for *you* to say something. I've waited two whole months." She paused. "This is the first time I've known you to keep secrets from me."

"I was embarrassed," I admitted. "I've never been evicted."

"I've been kicked out of worse places than this. Of course, that was before I married Mr. Moneybags. Millionaires don't get kicked out of places."

Mona had referred to her late husband, Henry Epps, as Mr. Moneybags even when he was alive. He'd thought it cute. But then, Mona had loved him despite his being much older. Plus, she claimed it was easier to get naked with a man twenty years her senior.

"You were too embarrassed to tell *me*?" Mona said. "I'm supposed to be your best friend."

"I knew you'd try to bail me out. It's my responsibility to take care of it." I paused. "I haven't even told Jay."

"When do you plan to tell him? Before or after we're kicked out on the street?"

"I told you how critical he has been since the . . . um, mishaps two months ago. I didn't want to give him more ammunition."

"Can you blame him for being worried?" she asked. "He wants you to be safe."

"I'm a lot safer than he is," I muttered. "I don't purposefully run into burning buildings."

"So where are we going to move?"

"We have a couple of options. The first one isn't really that desirable, but it's cheap."

"What makes it undesirable?"

"I think the bars on the doors and windows might scare prospective patients."

"What's the other option?"

I hesitated. "Thad Glazer offered to share his suite of offices."

Mona stopped me with one hand. "Wait, I think I misheard you. You were too embarrassed to tell Jay or me about the eviction, but you told Thad? And you're

willing to let *him* help you and not the two people closest to you?"

"I had no intention of telling Thad," I said, under-
standing why Mona might be hurt. "It just came out
while we were having lunch."

"You had lunch with Thad?"

"We had hot dogs at the hospital. Try not to read
anything into it, okay? It's strictly business," I added.
"He claims he has been looking to get a psychologist
in his office. You know Thad hates listening to people's problems."

"Yeah, he can be shallow."

"It would a good career move. I'd actually have patients who paid their bills."

Mona looked thoughtful. "I can definitely see the
benefits, as long as Thad doesn't try to hump you."

"He's hot for his receptionist, Bunny."

"Oh jeez. Thad is the only guy I know who would
hire somebody named Bunny." Mona was quiet for a
moment. "Well, this is probably a good time to tell you
that I was planning on giving my notice, anyway. I've
decided to go to nursing school."

I felt my jaw drop. "Wow," I managed to say after a
minute.

"Amazing, huh?" she said. "After all these years, I
finally found my calling."

"Wow," I repeated.

"It hit me right out of the blue."

I was still trying to wrap my head around it. "Does

this have anything to do with all those cute young nurses you mentioned?"

"I'll admit the thought crossed my mind, but I've sort of been trying to find my purpose in life. Everybody needs a purpose. Besides, the mall no longer holds my interest."

I had a sudden image of hell freezing over.

"And just think. I could wear those cute little uniforms and have lunch with Liam every day. We'd have more in common if I became a nurse. Maybe I could volunteer in the meantime."

"When would you start classes?"

"After the first of the year," she said. "I plan to hire a tutor to help me prepare for the entrance exam. But I catch on fast."

That much was true. I'd taught Mona the computer basics after she'd offered to come in and answer my phone as a favor, and before long she'd become an expert at online shopping. Still, I couldn't imagine her sticking an IV into a patient any more than I could imagine her buying sheets with a thread count of less than 1200.

"Have you told Liam?"

"I want to surprise him." She smiled. "So, are you going to accept Thad's offer?"

"I'm still thinking about it, but I don't have a lot of choices."

"Who is going to pack up this place and move it?"

"I need to form a plan."

"I hope it's a really fast plan," Mona said.

"I should probably tell Jay first."

She arched both brows. "You think?"

I arrived home with a bag of fast food and climbed from my car, but I didn't make it far before I heard a voice calling my name. I winced. I knew that voice. I turned and found my neighbor, Bitsy Stout, standing across the street with her hands on her hips, looking like she was ready for a bullfight. Bitsy and I had a history. It was not good.

I gave her my best fake smile. Her blue gray hair had been curled and lacquered into place so that not even tornado winds would muss it. "Hello, Bitsy," I said. "You're looking well."

"Cut the sweet talk. I found two piles of dog poop in my yard this morning," she said, her tone accusatory.

"Gee, and all I got was a lousy newspaper."

"I am tired of cleaning up after that ugly dog of yours."

I crossed the street and got in her face. "Don't call my dog ugly."

"Then you keep that mutt out of my yard or I'm going to report you for not adhering to the leash laws."

"My dog is *not* pooping your yard," I said.

"It's people like you, *renters*, who give good solid neighborhoods a bad name."

"It's not my fault that nobody but riffraff wants to live across the street from you," I said. Bitsy had made

48

my life miserable after my mom and aunt had designed a sculpture for my front flower bed. Bitsy had declared it pornographic, and the next thing I knew she had her holy-rolling church group picketing on my lawn. I'd agreed not to press charges in return for her sour cream crumb cake recipe, but she had yet to hand it over.

"If I catch your dog in my yard I'm going to shoot her with my pellet gun," she added.

"I dare you," I said, using what I considered my most menacing voice. "You don't want to go to jail, Bitsy. Do you know what they do to blue-haired ladies in jail?" Her eyes widened. "Put *that* in your pellet gun," I said.

I turned and marched across the street to my house. I was actually looking forward to seeing the dog in question. Mike was a small wirehaired mixed terrier with huge brown eyes. She'd followed me home from a walk two and a half months ago. There had been no collar so I'd assumed she was a stray. I had tagged her with the name Mike before checking down under. Being a sucker for animals, I'd let her inside during the night when a bad storm blew in, only to awake the next morning to find that she had birthed five puppies.

I had recently found a home for the last puppy, and Mike wasn't taking it well. She was clearly depressed. Instead of greeting me happily the minute I walked through the door, as she once had, I found her sleeping in her box in the laundry room.

"Guess what?" I said. I held up the bag. "Junk food!" I announced. "I even got you your own burger."

Mike opened her eyes, climbed from her box, and headed toward the back door. Jay had installed a doggie door so that she could go out when she needed. Luckily, my backyard was fenced in so I didn't have to worry about her wandering off. It was probably the only reason Mike hadn't run away in search of her puppies.

I unwrapped her cheeseburger, which I'd ordered plain, as I waited for her to return. "I knew you wouldn't be able to resist this," I said when she rejoined me. I held it close to her nose. "Yum-yum," I said.

She sniffed it a few times but lost interest and returned to her bed. I was at a loss as to what to do. She'd barely touched her food for a week. In fact, she'd done little more than sleep.

I sat on the floor beside the large dog pillow I'd bought her. "Look, I told you from the beginning we couldn't keep the puppies," I said, "and it's not like they don't have good homes. I was very selective."

Mike sighed.

I sighed.

Maybe I'd rushed things by giving away the last puppy, I thought, but the experience had been exhausting. It had taken Mona's housekeeper and me both to keep up with the mopping and disinfecting.

Mike closed her eyes, and I headed for the kitchen. I ate my burger and fries, but I couldn't stop worrying. Finally, I reached for the wall phone and called the only person I knew who could advise me. Dr. Jeff Henry was Mike's veterinarian, and one of my closest friends, even though we'd only met a few months ago. He'd been there for me *and* Mike the night her smallest puppy had died.

He answered after a couple of rings. "It's me," I said.

"Hi, Me. What's up?"

He had a smile in his voice, but he sounded tired. "Mike's depressed."

"Uh-oh."

"Plus, she hates me for breaking up her family."

"She doesn't hate you."

"Let's just say I'm not her favorite person right now."

"Is she eating?"

"Not much," I said. "She mostly sleeps."

"Is she taking in liquid?"

"A little. I'm worried about her, Jeff."

"She's probably worn out, Kate. Giving birth and caring for pups is no easy task. Sounds like a job for Super Vet. Why don't you drop her off at my office on the way to work tomorrow so I can have a look? It'll give you a good excuse to see me."

I smiled. I especially liked Jeff because our relationship was simple and uncomplicated, unlike the others in my life. Before Jay and I had decided to work on our marital issues, I'd had a very small crush on Jeff. Not only was he good-looking, he was one of the nicest people I knew. And I'd been lonely.

Then I'd discovered, quite by accident, that he was gay. He didn't know I knew, although I'd expected him to have confided in me by now. I'd certainly spilled my guts to him. My greatest concern was that he feared it would affect our relationship. I wanted him to give me the chance to prove my loyalty.

Okay, so, maybe our relationship was a little more complicated than I thought.

"How come you sound so tired?" I asked.

"The last few weeks have been incredibly busy."

"That's a good thing, right?"

"Except when pet owners call me in the middle of the night because their cat hurled a fur ball," he said.

"I know the feeling," I told him. "I sometimes get calls from patients in the middle of the night. You wouldn't believe how many people get depressed at two a.m."

"How are things going otherwise?" he asked.

I hesitated. "I should probably tell you I've been evicted from my office," I said, "due to the nitroglyc-erin incident. I've been trying to fight it for two months, but the long and the short of it is I have to be out by the end of the day on Friday."

"That's terrible! Is there anything I can do?"

"Yeah, you can go to bed early tonight and try to catch up on your sleep."

"Yes, Mother."

I hung up a few minutes later and changed into jeans and a blouse. The phone rang. Jay spoke from the other end. "I'm two blocks from your house," he said. "Mind if I drop by?"

The sound of his voice made the tiny hairs on the

back of my neck prickle, but I was surprised to hear from him after what he'd said that morning; and even more so since he'd felt the need to ask permission before he came over. "Sure," I said.

I heard him pull into my driveway. I hung up the phone and hurried to the front door. I watched him climb from his SUV and make his way toward me, a sexy smile on his face. It should have been against the law for a man to look that good in jeans. He paused at the door and dropped a quick kiss on my mouth. "You got a beer for a tired fireman?" he asked.

"Of course."

We went into the kitchen, and I headed to the refrigerator. I pulled out his favorite beer and handed it to him.

"You're not going to have one with me?"

"No, I just had dinner, and I'm full."

"I'm sorry about this morning, Katie," he said.

"The first session is usually uncomfortable," I told him.

He opened his beer and took a sip. "Where's Mike?"

"In her bed," I said. "She's still moping around. I'm going to drop her off at the vet on my way to the office tomorrow. He suspects she's just run down after the puppies."

"I'd better look in on her." Jay set his beer on the counter, walked into the laundry room, and turned on the light. Mike's tail thumped at the sight of him. "Hello, girl," he said, leaning over to pet her. Mike rolled on her back and Jay scratched her belly.

He spent a few minutes talking to her before turning off the light. We walked into the living room. Instead of sitting on the sofa and pulling me onto his lap, he sank into an overstuffed chair and leaned his head back.

"How was your day?" he asked.

"Mona has decided to become a nurse."

He looked amused. "For some reason I have a hard time imagining that."

"How about you? Anything exciting going on?" I felt as though we were simply trying to make polite conversation.

"Same old, same old. I ran errands, paid bills, washed clothes."

Jay worked twenty-four hours on and forty-eight hours off. He spent the first day catching up on his sleep; on the second day he took care of personal business, including me.

"Actually, I had to go in for a meeting. The guys grilled burgers out back, but you know what it's like trying to eat around there. You take one bite, and the bells go off. Half the time it's some kid yanking an alarm, showing off in front of his buddies."

I thought the legal system needed to crack down on people, mostly kids, who got a kick out of pulling alarm boxes. A false alarm wasted precious time in the event of a real fire; lives were sometimes lost.

"Since I wasn't on duty, I got to finish my burger."

"What was the meeting about?"

He hesitated. "We've had a few fires that look like they were set by the same person."

I decided not to tell him I already knew. "That doesn't sound good," I said.

"Yeah. Most likely some guy getting his rocks off."

He took a sip of his beer. I wanted to know more, but Jay would only think I was grilling him and things would get tense. I had a feeling there was going to be enough tension in the air after I told him about my eviction.

"Guess what?" I said, doing an excellent job of avoiding the subject. "I had to admit a patient to the psychiatric ward today. Guess who I ran into?"

"Your mother and aunt?"

"Very funny. Carter Atkins," I said. "He's an orderly, you know. Do you think he's odd?"

"I think he wrote the book on odd."

"Well, he obviously loves being a volunteer fireman, because he plans to study for the exam."

Jay gave me a funny look. "Carter isn't a volunteer fireman. He just hangs out at the station and gets on everybody's nerves. The guys put up with him because he helps with the chores."

"I didn't know."

"He's not likely to pass the exam. He has already flunked it several times. He's not that sharp, you know?"

I felt a wave of disappointment for Carter. "He said your new female probie was hot."

"Did I forget to mention Carter is also a blabbermouth?"

"I hear she's, um, busty."

"Yeah, well, that doesn't hold much weight if you can't get along with people."

"Oh?"

"Mandy—that's her name—expects preferential treatment." He drained his beer and set the can on the coffee table. "I trained under her father, who was captain when I joined the department ten years ago. He got hurt in a fire while trying to drag an unconscious teenager to safety. He ended up a big hero but had to take early retirement because of his injuries. He moved his family to West Virginia because he loved the mountains."

"Is that why she was hired?" I asked. "Because of her father?"

"Let's just say it worked in her favor."

"Is she any good?"

"She's not bad," he said. "She wanted to follow in her old man's footsteps. You know how that goes. She just needs to climb down from her high horse." He smiled. "We also got a new guy in from Texas who really knows his stuff. Ronnie Sumner," he added. "He's funny as hell. Actually, he's from Atlanta. He moved to Texas because his wife's family was there. When they divorced he decided to move back. He specifically asked to work with our engine company because he said he likes being where the action is."

The engine company Jay was with was one of the busiest in Atlanta. "Well, you guys do get plenty of action," I said.

Jay gazed at me quietly for a moment. "I could use a little action right now."

His sudden interest surprised me, and I wondered if he'd needed time to unwind before getting romantic on me. He joined me on the sofa, pulled me into his arms, and gave me a long, slow kiss. The center of my stomach turned soft. He slipped one hand beneath my bottom and began a slow massage. I went hot all over.

"If you play your cards right I might stay the night."

I convinced myself this wasn't a good time to tell him about my eviction notice and Thad's offer to share his office. I had avoidance behavior down to a fine art.

chapter 4

....

I was only vaguely aware of Jay climbing from the bed the next morning at what felt like an ungodly hour. I tried to open my eyes, but my lids wouldn't cooperate. "Do you want me to get up and make you breakfast?" I asked.

He chuckled and kissed me full on the mouth. "When did you learn to cook?" he asked.

I pried my eyes open. "I could make you instant oatmeal."

"I'll grab something on the way. Go back to sleep."

I closed my eyes. At seven, the alarm clock shook me awake. I fumbled for it and turned it off, then lay in bed and thought about the previous night; hot kisses, skin on skin, the joy of having Jay fill me. I'd lain awake long after he had fallen asleep, feeling guilty that I had not told him about the eviction.

I was still fretting over it when I arrived at Jeff's office with Mike. I noted the lines of fatigue on his face. "You don't look so good," I said.

"I haven't had much sleep," he confessed. "An overweight dachshund hurt his back jumping off the bed in the middle of the night. I could hear the little fellow yelping in the background, so I had no choice but to come in. I barely made it home before I got another call; a poodle that had been in labor for a while and wasn't getting anywhere. I had to come back and do a C-section."

"Are they okay?" I asked.

"They're in the back sleeping soundly, and I'm not." He gave a weary smile.

"Don't you think it's about time you looked for a partner?"

"Not a bad idea," he said. He glanced down at Mike. "Why don't you plan on picking up your little princess at the end of the day?" he said. "We'll give her the royal treatment."

I arrived at my office twenty minutes later and came to a dead stop inside the reception room. Mona's housekeeper, Mrs. Perez, was sitting in one of the chairs, a wad of tissue in one hand, a rosary in the other. It was obvious she'd been crying.

"What's wrong?" I asked.

"The worst possible thing has happened," she said.

Our conversation was cut short when Mona appeared with a cup of coffee. She was wearing a starched white nurse's uniform and white soft-soled shoes.

She glanced at me. "Bad news," she said, handing the trembling woman her coffee. "Mrs. Perez's grandson, Ricky, was picked up by the police as he was leaving for school this morning."

"Oh no!" I said. I'd only met sixteen-year-old Ricky a couple of times, but Mrs. Perez had told me he was an honor student who dreamed of becoming a doctor. "What happened?" I asked.

"The police are idiots," Mrs. Perez said, choking back a sob. "They've locked my grandson up like an animal."

"For what?" I asked.

Mona looked at me. "The cops accused him of beating a priest with a baseball bat."

"It's a big fat lie!" Mrs. Perez said. "My grandson would never lay a hand on Father Demarco. Ricky idolizes him."

I knew that Ricky and his family, as well as Mrs. Perez, were strict Catholics. "Did this Father Demarco actually say that Ricky beat him up?"

Mona shook her head. "He was unconscious when the EMTs arrived. He had to undergo emergency brain surgery, so he's not talking. A nun who lives on the property found him. She claimed she saw Ricky running from the back of the church as she was dressing."

Mrs. Perez pressed her lips together in irritation. "That nun is old and half blind."

"It's clearly a case of mistaken identity," Mona said.

"It's not fair," Mrs. Perez said. "Ricky grew up in that church, and he does volunteer work. He taught Father Demarco how to use a computer."

"Where is Ricky *now*?" I asked.

"He's in the detention center," Mona said. "I called my attorney. He's on the way over."

"My daughter, Mary-Margaret, is there waiting for the attorney to arrive," Mrs. Perez said. "She told me not to come."

"She didn't want you to become even more upset," Mona said. "Lewis will take care of everything."

Lewis Barnes was Mona's lawyer, and the best in town. He was also expensive. Since Mrs. Perez's daughter was a single mother who barely made ends meet, I had to assume Mona was covering the costs. "Mr. Barnes is highly capable and has a lot of connections," I said to Mrs. Perez. "I'm sure he'll have Ricky out in no time."

"I should be with my daughter," Mrs. Perez said, weeping into her tissue. "She's always had to do everything on her own."

Mona had told me that Mary-Margaret had been wild and irresponsible as a teenager, bearing two children out of wedlock before she was twenty years old, and disgracing her family in the process. Finally, Mary-Margaret turned her life around. She was hardworking and had been taking college courses for years in hopes of earning a degree. She and her mother rented a duplex. Living next door, Mrs. Perez was able to help out with her grandchildren when necessary.

"The police need to open their eyes and see what's happening to our neighborhood," Mrs. Perez said. "A gang called the Thirty-Eight Specials has all but taken over. Two weeks ago they beat Ricky within an inch of his life."

"Oh no!" I said.

She nodded. "He was just walking down the sidewalk minding his own business when a bunch of them jumped him. There were witnesses, but nobody, including Ricky, would tell the police anything because they're scared to talk."

"You're going to move out of that neighborhood," Mona said firmly.

Mrs. Perez looked sad. "It used to be a nice place to live. Everybody was close and looked out for each other." She began weeping again. "My grandson is probably scared to death. He has never been in trouble. Who knows what they'll do to him?" she added. "He can't afford to let his grades slip, because he is counting on scholarship money."

"Maybe you can talk to Ricky," Mona said to me. "He's going to need help getting through this."

Mrs. Perez turned pleading eyes to me.

"Of course I'll talk to him," I said; my heart grew heavy at the sight of her distress.

The phone rang and Mona picked it up. "It's Lewis Barnes," she said. She listened carefully and made notes. Finally, she hung up. "Ricky is being arraigned at two o'clock today," she said. "Lewis promised to have him home in time for dinner."

Mrs. Perez clasped her tissues to her heart. "Oh, thank God!"

"I could see him first thing tomorrow morning," I said. Mrs. Perez nodded.

"It's not over," Mona said after a moment, her tone gentle. "The nun is sticking to her story."

Mona sent Mrs. Perez home in a cab. I waited until we were alone before I confronted her about her wardrobe. "Okay, I give up. Why are you dressed as a nurse?"

Mona bopped herself on the forehead with the ball of her hand. "I completely forgot I was wearing it," she said, "what with all the commotion. What do you think?" She turned around so I could get a full view. She even wore white hose.

"Back to my question," I said.

"Well, I was lying in bed last night thinking about nursing school when I remembered the Halloween party Mr. Moneybags and I attended three years ago. We dressed as a doctor and nurse. Mr. Moneybags went as a gynecologist." She smiled at the memory. "You wouldn't believe how long it took me to find the dang thing. I searched the attic for two solid hours!"

"You *still* haven't answered my question," I said. "*Why* are you dressed as a nurse?"

Mona shrugged. "I thought it would be fun. This way I can see what it *feels* like being a nurse without actually being one."

"Oh." I'm sure there was some part of Mona that thought it made sense. "You're not actually going to perform any, um, nursing duties, right?" I said.

"Of course not." She sighed. "Do you have any idea of the sacrifices I'll have to make in order to become a nurse? Nurses don't wear fingernail polish."

"I'm glad you've thought it through."

The phone rang and Mona answered it. She offered it to me. "It's Thad."

I took the phone. "Edith Wright called," he said. "Marie is being a real pain in the ass. Edith is threatening to drop-kick her from the window of the psychiatric ward if we don't do something," he added.

"Oh great," I muttered. I could feel my stress meter overflowing, and I'd been at my office less than an hour.

"I'm on my way over now," Thad said.

"I'll meet you," I said, knowing I would have to cancel my first appointment of the day.

I drove to the hospital, thankful that traffic was not bad at that hour. I found Thad and Edith standing in the hall. Edith wore a dark scowl. They glanced up as I approached.

"Marie has been a naughty girl," Thad said.

"What has she done?" I asked.

Edith wasted no time. "Last night at dinner she claimed the food was filled with toxins and unfit for human consumption. She threw her tray on the floor."

Edith looked from me to Thad and back at me. "Good thing I wasn't here."

Thad and I exchanged looks.

"I've got a padded cell with her name on it," Edith continued. "If she wants to act ugly, that's going to be her new address. I don't deal with ugly."

"Where is Marie now?" I asked.

"She's confined to her room. I've got Debra sitting outside her door." Edith looked at me. "You've met Debra. Big black woman? Six foot three, two hundred and fifty pounds? Nobody gets by Debra."

"I've increased the dosage on Marie's Vistaril," Thad said.

Edith checked her wristwatch. "I have a meeting," she grumbled. "And here I was counting on having a good day."

I watched her disappear down the hall. "I don't think Edith is very happy with our patient *or* us," I said.

Thad looked bewildered. "Which is surprising since I went out of the way to be especially charming," he said.

"I'd better look in on Marie," I said. "When I get back to the office I'm going to contact the police and see if a missing persons report has been filed with her description."

"Good idea," he said. He glanced at his watch. "I have back-to-back appointments. We'll play catch-up later." He started down the hall, then turned. "Have you given any more thought to my offer?"

"How soon can Mona and I move in?" I asked.

Thad reached into his pocket, pulled out a key, and tossed it to me. I caught it in one hand and prayed I wasn't making a monumental mistake.

I found Debra sitting outside Marie's room reading *Jet* magazine. "I need to see my patient," I whispered.

The woman didn't look up from her magazine. "Okay, but if she starts singing about hound dogs and pickup trucks I'm going to throw her in a cold shower, clothes and all," she added.

Marie was lying on her bed. Her eyelids were heavy, and she seemed to be struggling to stay awake. She did not look happy to see me. "I hate this place," she said, her voice thick.

"You'd make things easier on yourself and everyone else if you'd settle down and give the medication time to get into your system."

"They just want to drug me so I'll be less trouble," she managed. "I know how it works."

"Who wanted to drug you in the past?" I asked.

She didn't respond.

"We're just trying to keep you calm until the new mood-stabilizing drug Dr. Glazer prescribed starts working. You should be feeling better in a couple of days."

"Not as long at Attila the Hun is running the show," she said and closed her eyes.

"You need to try to cooperate and not make trouble," I said. "It's best if you remain on Edith's good side."

"She has a good side?"

"I can't swear to it." Marie didn't hear my response because she had drifted off.

My eleven o'clock patient, Alice Smithers, suffered from dissociative identity disorder, otherwise, and more traditionally, known as multiple personality disorder. There were more people living in her head than in most Italian households. Alice had sought my help when she began having problems at her last job, where she worked as an accountant. Accusations of affairs and skimming money had resulted, and she was given two weeks to find another job. To top it off, Alice's new roommate, Liz Jones, was partying half the night with her boyfriend, trashing Alice's condo, and had even stolen her credit card. It hadn't occurred to me that Alice's confusion, bewilderment, and poor memory were due to MPD until it was almost too late for both of us. Liz Jones was actually one of Alice's alter personalities, and the abusive boyfriend had put Alice in the hospital and attacked me as well. We'd later discovered that Liz was skimming money, sleeping with Alice's boss, and blackmailing him.

In the land of mental health, Alice was known as the host personality. She hid her good looks beneath clunky eyeglasses and ill-fitting clothes in shades of brown. It was Mona's wildest dream that Alice would get well and gain some fashion sense in the process.

Liz Jones, on the other hand, dressed provocatively,

slept around, and was a reckless spender, which is why Alice had cut up her credit cards.

I invited Alice to take a seat on the sofa in my office, and after grabbing her file, I took the chair next to her. "How's our new senior accountant doing?" I asked, proud that Alice had not only landed a job with a prestigious firm but had climbed the ranks quickly.

She took a deep breath. "I like being challenged, but it can also be stressful. I'm constantly worried about losing time."

Losing time, sort of like an alcoholic blacking out, usually meant the appearance of an alter personality. "You're afraid Liz will show up and do something that will cause you to lose your job?" I asked.

"Yes. You know how she is."

I'd seen very little of Liz since Thad and I had been consulting on Alice's treatment plan. He'd prescribed a psychotropic drug and was seeing Alice every other week for med checks, but it was Liz Jones that showed up because she was hot for Thad. Since I served no purpose for her, she kept quiet during my sessions with Alice.

"What would Liz have to gain by getting you fired?" I asked. "It would create hardship for her as well."

Alice seemed to think about it.

"As for the other personalities, they have proved helpful. I can't see how they would pose a threat."

"Since I haven't met them, I have to take your word for it," she said.

The other personalities knew about Alice and had listened to our conversations, but Alice knew nothing about them.

"Like I said, Emily is very personable. I think she was a great asset during your job interviews, especially when you felt so depressed. And Sue was the one who scanned the employment classifieds, wrote a kick-butt resume, and mailed it out to more than a dozen companies. They both have your best interests at heart." Sue seemed to be the glue that held everything together when Alice became stressed and overwhelmed. Frankly, I wished I had someone like Sue in my life.

"I suppose I should feel relieved and appreciative that they are so eager to help me," Alice said, "but as we both know, not everyone has my best interests at heart."

We were back to Liz again. "I think you're giving Liz more power by fearing her," I said. "You're turning her into the monster beneath the bed."

"She *is* a monster!" Alice said. "She almost got us killed."

Alice had a valid point there.

"Have you been practicing your relaxation exercises and writing in your journal?" I asked. I had tried to impress upon her the importance of keeping a journal as a way of lessening her stress. Stress was one of the reasons Alice sometimes took a hike and allowed an alter to handle her problems.

"I listen to the relaxation tapes before I go to sleep

at night," she said, "but I get a little freaked writing in my journal since I'm not the only one making entries." She sighed. "It's not like I can hide my journal from them, you know?"

I gave a sympathetic nod. It would have been funny if the situation weren't so serious. I'd seen Alice's journal, including the entries made by Emily and Sue and even Liz. What was fascinating was that the handwriting was different and while one personality was right-handed, another could be a lefty. Also, each personality had a different outlook on life.

Emily's writing was curvy with tiny circles dotting her i's and with smiley faces waiting at the end of her sentences. Emily longed to get out more and socialize because she was extroverted. Alice's and Sue's handwriting were similar; very neat and precise. They both enjoyed reading and browsing in antique shops.

Liz's strokes were large and bold because she only used a black felt-tip pen; and she spouted a lot of four-letter words and complained bitterly about the lack of fun in her life. She resented the others and often spoke about getting even, leaving me to wonder if Alice was right. Liz might just be the monster beneath the bed.

chapter 5

....

"*Your mother called* during your session with Alice and Friends," Mona said as I stared into the back of the small refrigerator to see if I could find real food. "She said it was urgent."

Everything was urgent as far as my mother was concerned. "How come we never have anything to eat back here?" I asked, noting that the only edible objects were small packets of soy sauce. It reminded me of my refrigerator at home.

"Do you want me to run downstairs and buy you a sandwich?" Mona asked.

I imagined Mona standing in line wearing her nurse's uniform from what looked like the 1970s. "No." I closed the refrigerator.

"Have you made any decisions about where we're

going to move?" Mona asked. "I think I should order business cards or at least have an address on hand to give to your patients. Maybe we could only give the new address to those who pay their bills. Even better, we could only give the address to those we like." She looked thoughtful. "Uh-oh," she said. "That would leave us with nobody."

"That's not nice," I said. "You can't dislike people just because they have emotional problems that make them a real pain in the butt to deal with."

"Wanna bet?"

I ignored the comment. "As for where we're going, I've accepted Thad's offer. He's going to add a desk to the reception area for you." I held my breath. I hoped Mona wasn't going to lecture me, or I would be forced to repeat how desperate I was.

As if reading my mind, she smiled. "It'll be great working in a nice office," she said, "and I can't wait to meet Bunny. I'll bet she and I end up being best friends. We can go out to lunch and shop together. The three of us can have sleepovers."

"I knew you'd be crazy about the idea," I said, turning for my office.

"Just one more question," Mona said. "How are we going to get from here to there? Is Bunny going to give us a ride in her Barbie car?"

I gave Mona a smug look. "It just so happens I know a woman who owns a red monster-sized pickup truck," I said.

* * *

My mother answered on the first ring. "You're not going to believe this," she said as soon as I spoke from the other end.

"Try me."

"Trixie went out on a date with Eddie Franks last night."

Oh hell, I thought. "Really?" I said instead.

"I don't trust him," she said. "He's too slick for Trixie. Plus, if he's a patient of yours, I know he must be psycho to boot."

"Not all of my patients are psycho, Mom. And you don't know that he's a patient."

"I didn't just fall off the back of a turnip truck," she said, "and you know as well as I do that your aunt is dumber than cow dung when it comes to men. I don't think she's had a date in twenty-five years."

"Did Aunt Trixie say whether she had a good time?" I asked.

"She got up humming this morning. She never hums. I hope he didn't take her to a motel."

I was more concerned about Eddie taking my aunt to the cleaners.

"Mom, I don't think Aunt Trixie would go to a motel with a man she barely knows."

"Do you know the last time either one of us actually *did it*? We have urges just like everyone else, you know."

The last thing I wanted to hear about was my mother's and aunt's urges. "Mom—"

"She wouldn't even know to practice safe sex," she interrupted.

"Would she tell you if anything happened between Eddie and her?" I asked. "I've never known the two of you to keep secrets from each other."

"Oh, like she's going to admit to a one-night stand. In our day, only sluts did that sort of thing. We would never have carried on like you and Mona do today."

I let the comment slide. I often did that with my mother. "I think you're worried over nothing. And to be perfectly honest, it's really none of our business what Aunt Trixie does or does not do," I added, although I had every intention of interrogating Eddie Franks during his next appointment.

My mother gave a grunt. "If Trixie gets the clap it's going to be your fault."

I wondered if this was the best time to discuss my move. I realized I had no choice, because I was tired of feeling stressed and desperate. "Mom, I need a favor," I said. "I need to borrow your truck."

"Excuse me?"

"I'm moving to another office. I mostly need to move books and supplies and a couple of filing cabinets."

"And you want to use *my* truck! Are you crazy? I'm the only one who drives that truck. Anyway, why are you moving? Have you not been paying your rent on time? If you had stayed with Jay he could have helped you budget your money better."

I listened to her go on. I was lucky that before my father died he had instilled a lot of good stuff in me. He had convinced me that I could do anything I set my mind to. He had taught me to believe in myself, and, despite my mother's best attempts, she had never taken that from me. It wasn't that she was cruel. It was simply her way.

"I'm being evicted for blowing up my office," I said, knowing I was only giving her more ammunition. For some reason I didn't care.

Silence on the other end.

"Where are you moving to?" she finally asked.

"I'm going to share office space with Thad Glazer."

"That pervert ex-boyfriend who used you?"

"Yes, that's the one."

"Oh brother. What does Jay think about that?"

I hesitated but decided I had no choice but to be up front with her. "I haven't told him."

Again, silence. It was rare that I could render my mother speechless. I'll admit I was feeling proud of myself.

"He is never going to take you back now," she whispered.

"I have to be out this Friday."

"That's three days from now! Why did you wait until the last minute? What have you been doing all this time? Next thing you'll tell me is that you haven't even packed. No, don't tell me. I already know." She gave a long-suffering sigh.

"On second thought, I should probably hire

professional movers," I said. "It'll be quicker and a lot easier on everybody." I held my breath and waited.

"Don't be ridiculous! There is no way I'm going to stand by and allow you to pay an exorbitant amount of money to hire movers when your aunt Trixie and I are perfectly capable of packing and moving your office. We'll be there first thing in the morning with the boxes," she said. "I'll get your uncle and cousin to come in Friday morning to move the heavy stuff."

I felt a sense of dread. My cousin Lucien played in a band called the Dead Artists and had tattooed and pierced all his body parts. Although much younger than I was, he had never made a secret that he harbored incestuous thoughts. I shuddered to think about it.

"Just leave everything to me," my mother said.

We disconnected and I leaned back in my chair. I had clearly manipulated her. Since I was not a manipulative person, I struggled with guilt for a few minutes. It was what my mother would have most wanted for me.

I found Mona on the phone. I waited for her to finish the call. "The moving arrangements have been made," I said proudly.

"Well, that's a relief."

"How about we go to lunch? My treat."

Mona looked surprised. "Sure. Where are we going?"

"I don't care as long as it's close to the fire station. I feel like dropping by to say hi to Jay."

"That will take forever with the traffic."

I told her about the new probie with the large

breasts. "The problem is she's been there at least two weeks and Jay hasn't mentioned her. I had to hear it from someone else."

"Does he usually discuss new people coming in?"

"He often makes passing remarks. I suppose I should overlook it. They're dealing with what looks to be a serial arsonist."

"That's not good." She looked thoughtful. "I wonder just how big those breasts are?"

"There's only one way to find out."

I quickly made my way into my office and grabbed my purse. I found Mona standing beside the door leading from the reception room, her own purse in hand. "Ready to roll?" she said.

I tried to dodge as much traffic as I could while driving south toward the heart of the city where Jay's engine company was located. As with most metropolitan areas, downtown Atlanta was skirted with a number of rough neighborhoods where crime, including intentional fire setting, ran rampant. Condemned buildings waited months for demo crews; they were enough of a fire hazard without someone putting a match to them. Jay had chosen to work in a high-risk area because he felt that was where he was most needed. It was also the most dangerous.

A half hour later we pulled into an Arby's. I placed three orders at the window. Mona and I ate on the way.

"I'm sure the woman is qualified or she would never have been hired in the first place," Mona said.

"Jay said she was not bad, but I think hiring her had a lot to do with her father. He was the fire captain when Jay signed on."

We pulled into the parking lot of the fire station, and I parked. "Okay, we're going to pretend we were in the neighborhood and decided to surprise Jay with lunch."

"Like he's going to believe it?" Mona said.

"You got a better idea?"

We climbed from the car. I waved to a couple of men I knew who were in the process of polishing the fire truck in front of the building. A fire truck was called an apparatus, although I just called it a fire truck. Mona and I went inside where a blond thirtysomething-year-old man was spraying the apparatus floor, named as such because that was where they parked the apparatus. He obviously didn't see or hear us, because he turned and the cold spray hit our ankles. Mona gave a squeal.

He looked up and immediately stopped the flow of water. "Oh man, I'm sorry!" he said. "Hold on a sec and I'll grab a couple of towels."

"He's good-looking," Mona whispered.

"You're supposed to be keeping your eyes out for the hottie with the big boobs," I whispered back.

The man returned with two towels. "I'm really sorry about that," he said. "I wasn't paying attention." He looked at Mona. "Oh, I got your uniform wet."

"That's okay," she said, waving it off. "I'm not expected at the hospital today." We quickly dried our ankles and shoes. "Thanks," I said as we handed him the towel.

"Just don't tell the captain," he said jokingly. "I haven't been here that long."

I smiled. "It'll be our secret. By the way, I'm Kate Holly, Jay's, um, wife, sort of," I said. I introduced Mona.

"Ronnie Sumner," he said. We shook hands.

"I was told you really know your stuff."

He looked pleased. "That's good to hear," he said. "Jay's in his office."

Mona and I headed that way. "Did you see the muscles bulging in his arms?" she whispered.

"I thought you only had eyes for Liam."

"Well, now that I'm practicing to be a nurse, I pay attention to body parts. One of my classes will be anatomy."

Mona and I stopped outside Jay's office. I couldn't help but notice through the glass windows the blonde sitting on the other side of his desk.

Mona noticed, too. "Uh-oh, she *is* hot."

"I shouldn't have come," I said. "Maybe we could slip away unnoticed." I'd barely gotten the words out of my mouth before Jay saw us. He smiled and waved us in.

"Kate, this is a surprise," he said, coming to his feet as we stepped inside. "Hi, Mona," he added. "I heard you were planning on becoming a nurse. Nice uniform."

"Right now I'm just practicing," she said.

He nodded as though it made sense.

"Mona and I were in the neighborhood and thought we'd bring you lunch." I handed him the bag. The smile he gave told me he hadn't fallen for my story.

"That was thoughtful of you," he said. "Thanks."

The young woman remained seated as Jay introduced her as Mandy Mason. She was a knockout all right, and, like Carter had said, she was well-endowed, plus some. She had an athletic build and wore her hair short; obviously it was easier to care for that style in her job.

"Kate is a psychologist," Jay said, "and a darn good one at that. Mona is her assistant."

"Nice to meet you," Mandy said. She smiled, but there was an edge to her. A tough-as-nails attitude that I suspected came from training and working in a male-dominated field.

I noted the firefighter's handbook spread open on Jay's desk. "I can see you're busy," I said, trying to make my voice sound light and airy.

"Don't rush off on my account," Mandy said, even though she made no move to get up. "I've probably imposed on Jay's good nature as it is. I guess you could say he's sort of taken me under his wing."

Jay gave her an odd look, and I sensed all was not as it appeared. I wished I hadn't come. "We can't stay," I said quickly. "I have a patient due in shortly." I looked at Mandy. "It was nice meeting you."

"Same here, Karen," she said.

"Kate," I corrected.

Jay rounded the desk. "Let me walk you to your car."

"No, no," I said, wanting to get out of there as quickly as I could. "Some patients get antsy if I'm not waiting for them the minute they arrive."

"Kate is right," Mona said. "I'll probably have to take their blood pressure."

Mona obviously sensed my urgency to escape; she and I bumped into one another trying to squeeze through the door at the same time, which made me feel even more foolish. Finally, we cleared the doorway and left the building.

"Holy hell!" Mona said once we'd climbed into my car. "I wonder if she has to carry a separate insurance policy on those things."

I pulled from the parking lot and headed north. "Do you think they're real?" I asked.

"Are you kidding? Silicone doesn't come in that size."

"Which explains why Jay didn't tell me about her," I said.

"You don't know that."

"Oh yeah? Did you notice how uneasy he was?" I asked. "He treated me like I was a casual acquaintance. What does that tell you?"

"I don't think it was us. I got the impression he felt uneasy with Mandy. Still, I've got a funny feeling about her."

I braked at a red light. "What do you mean?"

"You know how some women don't make friends with other women?" she said. "I'll bet she doesn't have one girlfriend. I don't trust her."

"I don't trust either damn one of them," I blurted, wondering if Jay had been thinking of Mandy as we'd made love the night before. I gritted my teeth and began doing multiplication tables in my head.

I tried to disguise my bad mood behind a fake smile as I greeted my next appointment, a couple I was seeing for marriage counseling. I seemed to be doing a lot of couple's therapy these days, which was ironic since Jay and I were in counseling as well.

The couple had enjoyed twenty-five years of marriage until the wife found her husband's stash of dirty pictures in the bathroom, tucked between the pages of his hunting and fishing magazine. She had taken it personally. She was angry and hurt and all of the above. She'd even moved out of the bedroom. Finally, she had admitted they'd gotten into a rut, both in their relationship and sex life.

I had given them homework. They'd each made a list of what had attracted them to each other in the beginning. Their lists were long; just thinking about what it had felt like falling in love so many years ago had put a glow on both of their faces. They were now setting up a real date for the end of the week.

I felt confident it wouldn't be long before they were

sharing the same bed again. I didn't feel so confident about Jay and me.

I was getting ready to leave for the day when Edith Wright called with more complaints about Marie.

"She told the other patients we were trying to poison them with medication. I'm telling you, the woman is so manic she's almost bouncing off the wall. If she refuses to take her Vistaril tonight, I'm going to slap her silly."

I knew Edith was just venting. "I don't think that's allowed," I said.

"I'll try not to leave any marks."

"How about I ask Dr. Glazer to speak with her," I said.

"That might work, what with his silver tongue. Lord knows it works on the nurses."

chapter 6

·····································

I made it to Jeff's office shortly before closing time.

The technician called me back, and I found Jeff standing beside the stainless steel exam table petting Mike. He smiled, but it did little to erase my pissy mood or the exhaustion on his face. He wasted no time with the usual pleasantries.

"I drew some blood, and other than being a little anemic, Mike is fine," he said. "I'm putting her on a regimen of B-12 vitamins. I also gave her an injection to jump-start the process. If you don't notice an improvement in a week to ten days, I want to see her again. What are you feeding her, by the way?"

"Dog food."

He laughed. "What *kind* of dog food?"

"Whatever is on sale when I go to the store," I confessed.

"I've got something out front that meets the daily vitamin requirements and promotes a healthy immune system. I'll sell it to you at cost."

"I can't let you do that, Jeff."

"Yes, you can. I'm not in the dog food business."

"Okay, I'll agree to be your charity case," I said, "but only if you promise to get some rest. Mike and I need you. Plus, you're the only one who knows I can eat an entire pint of Ben and Jerry's in one sitting."

Out front, I paid the bill, noting that Jeff had cut me some slack on that as well. As I waited for my receipt to print out, the receptionist answered the phone. She immediately motioned for the technician.

"Mel Giddings's German shepherd was just hit by a car. He's on his way over with Max now."

"Oh no!" the tech said. "Did he say how badly Max was injured?"

"He was so upset I could barely understand him."

"I'll tell Dr. Henry and get the OR ready in case we have to do surgery." She hurried away.

"It doesn't look like your boss is going to catch up on his rest anytime soon," I said, feeling as bad for Jeff as I did for the poor dog.

She shook her head sadly as she handed me my receipt. "I don't know how the man does it," she said, "but sooner or later it's going to catch up with him."

I led Mike to the car and helped her inside. Instead of driving home, I stopped by a fast-food restaurant and ordered chicken fingers and fries for myself and a plain burger for Mike. I drove to the park near my house. I hoped the fresh air would improve my mood. I was probably overreacting about Mandy, but a small voice in my head told me it would explain why Jay had become standoffish the past few weeks. I tried to ignore the voice.

I found a bench, and once Mike was situated beside me, I offered her the burger. She turned her nose up at it. I tried to get her interested in a chicken finger; she ignored it as well.

"That stuff will kill your dog," a woman's voice said.

I turned and found an elderly lady sitting on a bench nearby holding a tiny Yorkie on her lap. The woman had cotton white hair and wore a starched sky blue dress. "It's just chicken," I said.

"Yes, but you don't know what kind of oil it was fried in," she said. "You eat that, and you'll need a plunger to get the clogs out of your arteries."

I looked at the chicken. Surely it would have come with a warning label if it was as dangerous as the woman claimed. I suddenly remembered the bag of healthy food I'd purchased for Mike and made a solemn promise to start her on it as soon as I got home.

"I should probably mind my own business," the woman said, "but your dog doesn't look well to begin with."

"She had puppies a couple of months ago," I said. "Her vet said she's anemic. He's got her on special vitamins."

"Oh, what do they know?" she said. "I prefer a

holistic approach. She's probably suffering from post-partum depression. I have a friend who is really good at helping mama dogs through that sort of thing."

"Really?"

"And if you want her to live a long life you have to feed her wholesome foods. I am very particular about what I feed my Prissy." She suddenly smiled. "I'll bet your pooch would love to have one of Lila's love treats," she said.

"She doesn't have much of an appetite these days," I told her.

The woman put her Yorkie on the bench beside her. "Now, Prissy, I want you to sit still so Mama can take a look at this nice lady's poor, sick animal." She pulled a plastic bag from her purse and glanced at me. "What is your dog's name?"

"Mike."

"You gave her a boy's name? What a cute idea!" She walked over to Mike and smiled. "Hello, there, young lady. My name is Lila Higginbothom. Would you like to try one of my special treats?" She held out a small biscuit.

Mike gave a dainty sniff before snatching it between her teeth and wolfing it down.

I couldn't hide my surprise. "She ate it!"

"Dogs love Lila's love treats."

I looked more closely at the woman. Her face was webbed with soft wrinkles. She had kindly blue eyes. I stuffed my snack pack inside the sack and stood. "You'll have to tell me where I can buy them," I said.

She waved off the comment. "Oh, I make them myself. I use only organic products, and I always add virgin coconut oil because you can't go wrong with coconut oil. It has so many healthy benefits, you see. I can give you all the treats you want."

Mike wagged her tail frantically, eyeing Lila's plastic bag. "I'll be more than happy to pay for them," I said, relieved that Mike had finally eaten something.

"Oh, I wouldn't think of charging you," she said. "It's my pleasure."

I laughed. "I think she wants another one."

"Well, of course she does," Lila said, giving Mike a second biscuit. Again, Mike ate as though she couldn't get enough.

"Here, take the bag," Lila said, offering it to me. "And write down my phone number for when you need more. I make a fresh batch once a week."

"I'd love to have your recipe," I said, although I had no idea if the oven worked at my place. If food didn't go into a microwave, I didn't buy it.

"Oh, it's a secret," Lila said, almost whispering the words.

She waited until I had written down her phone number. "Does Mike have toys?" she asked.

"She has a couple, but she hasn't felt much like playing. And I buy her rawhide bones."

Lila shuddered. "Oh, some of those bones are so nasty you may as well feed her tire rubber. I suggest you buy her only those bones that remove tartar buildup; otherwise, you're going to spend a fortune having her teeth cleaned."

"I didn't know dogs actually had their teeth cleaned," I said.

"I brush Prissy's teeth with beef-flavored toothpaste." She studied Mike closely. "I think you should arrange playdates for her."

"Playdates?"

"Dogs are very social animals. She needs to be able to interact with other dogs. I try to set up playdates for Prissy a couple of times a week."

"Gee, I had no idea having a pet was so involved. I wasn't allowed to have a dog while I was growing up because my mother is afraid of them. I guess I have a lot to learn."

"I have an excellent idea!" Lila said. "You could bring Mike over tomorrow to play with Prissy. We would love to have her, wouldn't we, Prissy?" The Yorkie wagged her tail from the other bench as though she knew exactly what Lila was saying. "Where do you live, dear?" she asked me.

I wasn't keen on giving strangers my address, even though Lila seemed harmless enough. I told her the general area.

"Why, you're only a few miles from me," she said. "Why don't you drop Mike off in the morning? She can spend the day with Prissy. We'll have a grand old time!"

Lila didn't hesitate to give me her address. I felt silly for holding back my own. I suppose it had to do with my line of work, and the fact that, as Jay had reminded me more than once, I seemed to draw odd people like a magnet.

"That's very kind of you to invite Mike," I said.

She waved off the remark. "I'm a sucker for animals. Once your little pooch spends the day playing with Prissy, you'll see a big improvement."

Mike seemed in better spirits as I drove home. She was sticking her head out the window and catching the breeze, which had turned cold. I shivered but left the window down since it was the first time in days I'd seen Mike interested in anything but sleeping.

I, on the other hand, was feeling overwhelmed. Instead of counting red lights, I counted dollar signs. When had pets become so expensive? I pulled into the driveway and helped Mike from the car. She followed me as I dumped the burger and chicken snack in the trash and filled her bowl with the food I'd purchased at Jeff Henry's office. I was surprised when she began to eat hungrily.

"Wow," I said. "Your mood sure has improved." She wagged her tail and gave a huge yawn, then went to her bed and lay on her back in a most unladylike fashion.

"I need to run out and pick up those special bones so you don't have tartar buildup," I told her. "Next thing I know you'll need braces." But Mike was already snoring.

I arrived at the Walmart Supercenter with a list in my head. At the pet department, I read the ingredients on the packaged bones and chose several that promised to promote good dental health.

I hurried across the store to the food section, where the smell of whole roasted chickens beckoned me. I grabbed a bag of premixed salad greens and several tomatoes from the produce section before making my way to the dairy section and finally, to the frozen food case. I passed by the high-calorie, high-fat frozen dinners and chose several healthy ones instead. I tried to ignore the pints of Ben and Jerry's ice cream crying out to me, and I would have been less tempted had Walmart not been running a sale. I bought six pints of Chocolate Fudge Brownie. I can be weak like that.

I'd arrived back home and put away the few groceries I'd purchased when the doorbell rang. I found Jeff Henry standing on the threshold.

"I forgot to give you Mike's vitamins," he said, holding up the plastic container.

"You didn't have to drive over," I said. "I would have picked them up." I frowned. "Are you okay?" He didn't look okay; he looked ready to drop.

"I just spent three hours performing surgery on a German shepherd."

"How is he doing?"

"He'll make it, but I'm going to have to check on him several times during the night. I figured I'd grab a sandwich and a cup of coffee in the meantime, but I wanted to drop off these vitamins first."

"Come inside," I said sternly. "I bought a roasted chicken. I can make you a sandwich."

"Coffee, too?"

"Uh-huh."

He stepped inside. "You're a saint."

"Yeah, yeah," I said. "Have a seat on the sofa, and I'll put the coffee on."

"Please make it strong," he said, sitting down and leaning his head back against a cushion. "It's going to be another long night."

I went into the kitchen, where I put the coffee on and pulled the chicken from the refrigerator. I cut several slices from the breast for a sandwich. Once the coffee was ready, I carried a steaming mug and a small plate containing a sandwich into the living room. Jeff was sprawled on my sofa, out cold. I pondered waking him but decided against it. Even a small nap would help revive him. I carried his food and coffee back to the kitchen.

The phone rang, and I hurried to answer so it wouldn't wake Jeff. Jay was on the other end of the line.

"I'm calling to thank you for lunch today," he said.

I wondered if he were feeling guilty or wanted to see if I had something to say about Mandy. I decided to keep my mouth shut. "You're welcome," I whispered.

"Why are we whispering?" he whispered.

"Mike's vet dropped off her vitamins and fell asleep on my sofa while I was making him a sandwich."

"Should I be jealous?"

"Of course not." I hadn't told Jay that Jeff was gay. For some reason I felt it would be a betrayal to a man who had become a good friend. "The poor guy hasn't had a decent night's sleep since I don't know when. He just conked out on me."

"Is he spending the night?"

"Why would you ask that?"

"I'm teasing, Katie. What did he say about Mike?"

"He thinks she's worn down due to the puppies. He put her on vitamins. I took her to the park this evening. I met a very nice elderly lady named Lila. She invited Mike over to play with her Yorkie tomorrow. She said Mike needed a playmate."

"I would never have thought of that," he said.

"Lila is an expert on dogs."

"It sounds like it."

"Um, Jay, I need to talk to you about something," I said, knowing I had to come clean with him once and for all about my office move. I'd put it off long enough.

"Sounds serious," he said. "I'm listening."

"I'd rather talk in person."

"Are you okay, Katie?" He sounded concerned.

"I'm fine. It's just . . . well, I agree that I need to be more open."

"You can talk to me anytime, Katie."

I started to answer, but the sudden sound of loud, piercing bells stopped me.

"Well, maybe not this minute," he said. "I have to go."

The next thing I heard was a dial tone. I hung up. I heard a noise behind me and turned. Jeff was standing in the doorway, disheveled and rubbing his eyes.

"I'm sorry I fell asleep on your sofa."

"You were exhausted." I got up and motioned for him to take a seat at the table. "The coffee is still hot, and I made a sandwich for you."

"You're too good to me."

I set the coffee mug in front of him. "I think a little pampering is in order after all your hard work." I handed him the plate with his sandwich.

"You didn't trim the crust?" he asked.

"Don't push it, Jeff." I poured a cup of coffee for myself and joined him.

He took a bite of his sandwich and chewed. "Wow, this is a great sandwich. This might just be the best sandwich I've ever had."

"I'm a marvel in the kitchen."

"No wonder Jay fell madly in love with you."

I stared into my coffee cup.

"Uh-oh. Did I say something wrong?"

"Jay and I are in marriage counseling. We seem to have so many issues." I sighed.

"I'm sure the two of you will work it out," he said. "Everybody has issues. Take me, for example. Do you know how much I hate having to express an animal's anal glands? And I'm a vet, for Pete's sake! It's in my job description."

I laughed. The good thing about Jeff was his sense of humor. "That is so gross. Don't you have someplace you need to be, Dr. Henry?"

"Yeah, I'd better go check on my patient. What do I owe you for the sandwich and coffee?"

"Get out of here."

We both stood. I walked him to the door. He kissed me on the forehead. I realized, as I watched him pull from the driveway, how much I appreciated his friendship. It bothered me that I was able to spill my guts to him so easily but knew very little about him. He kept a lot to himself. I was reminded that Jay had accused me of the same thing, but it seemed I wasn't the only one holding back.

chapter 7

I awoke early the next morning, and no matter how hard I tried, I could not go back to sleep. I trudged downstairs, poured a cup of coffee, and turned on the early morning local news. It seemed Atlanta never rested; there had been car accidents and crimes committed as I'd slept. Fire had gutted an apartment complex north of town. Fortunately, there were no casualties. Firefighters answered a lot of calls, many just as dangerous as the apartment complex, but only the big ones made the news.

As I sipped my coffee, I mentally rehearsed how I would break the news to Jay about my eviction and my decision to share an office with Thad. Jay was not an unreasonable man; surely he would see that the move was good for my career. Plus, he knew Thad and I shared patients from time to time. He would understand my decision.

I turned off the TV and went into the kitchen, where I refilled my cup. Mike came into the room, looking as though the weight of the world were on her shoulders. And she had seemed to be doing so much better the day before. Wouldn't it be just my luck to have a bipolar dog, I thought. I saw her staring at the plastic bag of treats on the counter, and I gave her one. She gobbled it and headed out her doggie door for her morning business.

I showered and dressed, then called Lila to make certain she was still expecting Mike.

"Prissy is very excited," she said.

I led Mike to the car. Her mood had changed for the better; she loved riding in the car. Perhaps Lila was right. Maybe Mike needed a friend, just as I had needed one the night before. I thought of Jeff and hoped he'd gotten some sleep.

Lila lived in a duplex with a neat lawn and well-tended flower beds. Mike and Prissy sniffed each other as I chatted briefly with Lila in her cozy living room. I noted an odd smell.

"I'm baking my famous love treats," Lila said as though reading my mind. "Prissy and I are early risers. Be sure to remind me to send a batch home with you when you pick up Mike at the end of the day."

Prissy was intent on licking Mike's ear clean. "I guess they've bonded," I said.

Lila smiled. "Prissy loves making new friends.

Now, get on with you and don't worry about a thing. I've got a full day planned for our little ones."

I arrived at my office, where Mrs. Perez and her grandson waited. He was slender, dressed in jeans and a football jersey. He stood as I approached. Obviously somebody had taught him good manners.

"Hi, Ricky," I said, offering my hand. He'd gotten taller since I had last seen him. "Nice to see you again," I added.

"Same here, Dr. Holly," he said politely.

Mona wasn't at her desk. I didn't know if she was making coffee or giving health exams down the hall.

I exchanged a few pleasantries with Mrs. Perez, then invited Ricky inside my office. I was about to close the door when Mona showed up with a tray containing three cups of coffee and a bottled water. I tried not to stare at the additions she'd made to her uniform, a nurse's cape and cap. She handed the water to Ricky.

"Thank you, Nurse Clara Barton," I said.

She gave me an odd look; obviously she had no idea who Clara Barton was.

I invited Ricky to take a seat on the sofa. I sat in my chair. "I hear you're going through a rough time," I said. "How are you doing?"

He shrugged. "I'm hanging in there. My mom said to thank you for seeing me. She would have been here if she could, but it's hard for her to get off work. Plus, she's taking a couple of night classes and studying for an exam."

"What is her major?"

"Elementary education," he said. "She has always wanted to be a teacher. She taught my sister and me to read before we started school."

"How old is your sister?"

"She just turned fifteen."

I smiled. "Do the two of you get along or do you argue like most brothers and sisters?"

"We're pretty tight," he said.

I took a sip of my coffee and set my cup on the table beside me. I could tell he was nervous. "Your grandmother thought it would be good if you had someone to talk to while you're going through this difficult time," I said. "I'm sure it must be very stressful."

"I didn't beat up Father Demarco like the police accused me."

"How is he?"

"My grandmother called the hospital last night. He's still critical."

"I understand the two of you are close."

"I've been an altar boy since I was in fifth grade. I do volunteer work for the church. Father Demarco is helping me look for scholarships."

"You want to be a doctor, eh?" I asked.

"I plan to be a regular GP and open a clinic one day for people who can't afford decent medical care. Unless I go to prison," he added. "The prosecutor wants me tried as an adult. Mr. Barnes is fighting it."

"That must be scary for you."

Ricky nodded but said nothing.

"Who do you think attacked Father Demarco?" I asked.

"I don't know."

"Does anyone have a grudge against him?"

"I can't think of anyone. He's just an old priest who likes helping people."

"Your grandmother thinks it was gang related. She says some members of a gang beat you up two weeks ago."

"I don't know that they were in a gang. My sister and I were walking home from the bus stop, and a couple of guys started messing with her. I told them to cut it out, and that's how the fight started."

"If you knew they were in a gang, would you tell?"

He shook his head. "They'd come after me."

"Why do you suppose the nun told the police it was you?" I asked.

"Maybe the person who did it resembled me. That's the only thing I can think of. She's really old. Her eyesight isn't good."

We were both silent for a moment. "How can I help you, Ricky?"

"You could tell the judge you don't think I did it."

"I can't do that. The only thing I can do is act as a fact witness. I could tell the court you appeared for all your sessions, but I can't act as a character witness. The court would have to appoint someone."

He gave a huge sigh. "I need to get to school," he said. "I have a third-period geometry test."

"Why don't we schedule another appointment?" I suggested.

He hesitated. "I'm not sure what good it would do, and I don't want to waste your time."

"I'm a good listener, Ricky, and your mother and grandmother would probably feel better if you had someone to talk to," I added. "Everything would be confidential, of course."

He seemed to consider it. "I hate to see them worry so much. Maybe I could come in after school."

We set up a time. I walked Ricky out. Mrs. Perez shot me a questioning look, but I avoided meeting her gaze as I checked with Mona to make sure she hadn't scheduled an appointment in the slot I'd given Ricky. He followed his grandmother out.

"Lewis Barnes called," Mona said. "He had both good news and bad. I didn't tell Mrs. Perez."

"What did he say?"

"The good news is he convinced the prosecutor to try Ricky as a juvenile."

"What's the bad news?"

Mona hesitated. "They found the bat that was used to beat Father Demarco. Ricky's fingerprints were all over it."

chapter 8

·····································

I felt like someone had just punched me in the stomach. I sank into one of the chairs. "Are they sure?" I asked.

"The police fingerprinted Ricky when they booked him. The prints were a perfect match."

"Well, then," I said, not knowing what else to say. "That sort of changes things," I added.

"Kate, I've known Ricky for years. He's not a violent person. I still think he's being framed."

"Doesn't sound like the evidence supports that, Mona."

"All I'm asking is that you give him the benefit of the doubt," she said. "He may have a perfectly good explanation."

"It's not up to me," I said. "I'm not the one prosecuting him. I just remembered, I need to call the police department and talk to someone in missing persons," I said, wanting to change the subject. "I'm hoping somebody is looking for Marie." I turned for my office.

"I'll call," Mona said.

I thanked her and went into my office. I was still trying to come to terms with what I'd learned about Ricky Perez when my mother called. "Trixie didn't come home last night," she said. "That's not like her. I've checked with the police department and all the hospitals. I just know Slick Eddie has done something bad to her."

"Mom, don't you think you're overreacting?" I said, although it didn't sound good. But I didn't want her to fret. I planned to confront Eddie the next time I saw him.

"I feel it in my bones, Kate. Twins are like that. You're going to have to level with me since I know Slick Eddie is a patient of yours. Is he a pervert?"

"It would be unethical for me to tell you whether or not he's a patient," I said. "But having met him, I have no reason to believe he's a pervert."

She sighed. "I'm still worried about her."

"Let's not automatically assume the worst," I said, only to remind myself that I had misjudged Ricky and may have done the same with Eddie Franks.

"I'll be there shortly to start packing your office," she said before we hung up.

I checked my watch. I still had a few minutes before my next patient arrived. I reached for a legal pad and jotted brief notes about my session with Ricky Perez.

No matter what the evidence proved, it was still hard to believe that he was guilty of attacking a priest, especially one who had acted as his mentor.

Mona peeked in. "I checked with missing persons. They don't have anyone who fits Marie's description, but they promised to keep an eye out. Are you okay?"

I looked up. "I have a lot on my mind."

She sat on the sofa. "Have you told Jay about you-know-what?"

"I told him we needed to talk. But I'd rather tell him in person."

"How do you think he'll take the news?"

"He's not going to like it," I said. "It's just going to add to the stress of our relationship." I sighed. "I can't believe people actually pay me to help them solve their problems when I have so much trouble solving my own."

"I have a question, and I want you to answer it honestly," she said.

"Okay," I said, waiting for the worst.

"Does it bother you that I'm wearing a nurse's uniform? I mean, I don't have to wear it to work. I can just wear it around the house."

I chuckled. "No, it doesn't bother me. Just be careful if my aunt Lou shows up, because you know how she is. She'll expect you to treat her vaginitis."

Mona shuddered. "I don't even want to *think* of that woman's vagina. It gave birth to your sicko cousin, Lucifer."

"Lucien," I corrected.

"I keep getting his name mixed up because he looks like he should be the gatekeeper in hell."

I had to agree.

I called the hospital and asked for Edith Wright. I was put on hold. Finally, she picked up.

"Good morning, Edith," I said. "It's Kate Holly."

"I'd planned to call you as soon as I got caught up. It's been a madhouse this morning. Oops, I probably shouldn't have used that word. Anyway, your patient hit the skids. She literally crashed overnight, but you learn to expect these things with bipolar patients."

"How bad is she?"

"If it gets much worse I'll have to put her on suicide watch."

"Oh no! Have you spoken with Dr. Glazer?"

"I left a message with that dingbat secretary of his. I had to spell my name three times before she got it. I was tempted to drive over there and slap her silly."

"I'll put a call in to Dr. Glazer right now."

"Thanks," Edith said. "It'll be one less thing."

I dialed Thad's office and asked to speak to him. From the other end of the line, Bunny gushed. "Oh, Dr. Holly, Thad told me you and your receptionist plan to move in this Friday. We are going to have so much fun!"

"Mona and I are looking forward to it," I said.

"If you can hold two teeny-weeny seconds, I think Thad is finishing up with a patient."

Thad picked up a moment later. "I was just thinking about you," he said. "Are you wearing underwear?"

I ignored him. "Our patient has crashed and burned."

"Uh-oh."

I repeated what Edith had told me. "I've got a patient due in any minute. As soon as the session ends, I'll drive over and check on her."

"You've got my cell if you need me."

Stanley Glick had only been in a couple of times. I liked Stanley because he paid his bill after each visit. His wife, also his business partner in a successful real estate company, had sent him packing after twenty-five years of marriage due to a midlife crisis of his that had come with a seventy-thousand-dollar Mercedes sports car and a blonde half his age.

Stanley had been too busy with his new girlfriend to give much thought to the woman who'd raised his children. That is, until she'd met someone.

"I can't believe Doris actually invited another man to have dinner at our house and in front of our children," he said.

"The two of you are divorcing," I reminded him. "Don't you think she has a right to move on with her life?"

"She's only doing it to get back at me. Did I tell you she joined the gym and lost fifteen pounds?"

"I believe you mentioned it." Stanley and his wife had worked out a schedule to avoid running into each other at their office until they decided what to do with the business. But he'd had to go by a couple of times to pick up a forgotten file or meet with a new client. I suspected he was doing it on purpose. Now Stanley was losing interest in the girlfriend.

"Doris bought a whole new wardrobe," he said. "She wears tight skirts and low-cut blouses. I don't know what has come over her."

It didn't take a rocket scientist to figure out that Stanley Glick was still in love with his wife. I wasn't sure he was aware of it, but it would be interesting to see how things turned out.

My mother and aunt showed up shortly before ten o'clock with packing supplies. I noticed my aunt was glowing, and I hoped she hadn't already fallen in love with Eddie Franks.

"Sorry we're late," my mother said. "Trixie didn't arrive home until an hour ago." She shot my aunt a dark look.

"Guess what Eddie and I did last night?" Aunt Trixie said, grinning like a teenager.

I smiled. "Tell me."

"We played all-night bowling. And I'm not even tired!"

My mother pursed her lips. "All-night bowling, my foot," she muttered.

Trixie looked hurt. "What's wrong with you, Dixie? Why are you so against me having a little fun? Why, they even have senior citizen leagues during the week. You and I—"

"We have a business to run," my mother said, "or have you forgotten?"

Trixie looked hurt. "Having our own business does not mean we can't take a little time off to enjoy life."

While I hoped my mother and aunt weren't going to get into a long-winded argument, I had to applaud Trixie's spunk.

My mother ignored her and looked at me. "Where do you want us to start?"

I looked about. "You can begin packing the books in my office," I said. "I have to go to the hospital."

My mother looked concerned. "What's wrong with you?" she said. "Are you ill? You can tell me, you know. If you're sick you'll have to move in with us so I can take care of you."

"I'm seeing a patient, Mom."

"Oh, for Pete's sake!" she said. "Why didn't you say so? Why do you have to scare me like that, Kate?"

"You do it to yourself," I said.

"She's right, Dixie," my aunt said. "You're always jumping to conclusions, and most of the time you're wrong."

My mother was clearly insulted. "What do you know? If you had a brain you wouldn't be out gallivanting all night with some man who has serious psychiatric problems and should probably be locked in a nut ward for the rest of his life."

Trixie looked at me. Her bottom lip trembled. "Is that true?"

"No. Mr. Franks is as sane as we are." It wasn't until

after I'd said it that I realized I should have used a better example. Most of my family and friends straddled the line between normal and abnormal. As if to prove that point, Mona came out of the bathroom in her nurse's uniform.

Trixie and my mother stared openly. "Oh, Mona, when did you become a nurse?" Trixie asked.

I figured it was a good time to slip out.

I found Marie lying on her bed facing the wall. I touched her shoulder. "I hear you're having a bad day, Marie," I said. "Is there anything I can do?"

She rolled over and faced me. "My name isn't Marie, but you already know that. Sometimes, when I experience mania, I hallucinate. As for feeling crappy as hell, I've been to the dark side of manic-depressive illness before."

I couldn't hide my surprise. She may have been depressed, but she was clearly lucid. "Will you tell me your real name?"

"Elizabeth Tyler Larkin. My husband is Senator John Larkin of Vermont."

"Wow." I suddenly realized why she looked familiar to me. I'd seen a photo of her and the senator on the front page of a tabloid some time ago while I was standing in line at the grocery store. I vaguely remembered the caption; something about her husband abusing an employee—the housekeeper, as I recall.

Elizabeth got up from the bed, walked into the

bathroom, and splashed water on her face. As my memory was jogged, I also remembered the senator giving a news conference in front of his home where he'd vehemently denied accusations of throwing a glass dish at the woman. Elizabeth had stood beside him but had remained quiet. The news had died down within a few days; the housekeeper had dropped charges and conveniently disappeared. I'd suspected she had been paid off.

Elizabeth returned and sat on the edge of her bed. "I would appreciate it if Dr. Glazer would cut back on the dosage of whatever sedative he has been giving me. I don't want to be drugged. I've spent the last year so doped up I could barely get out of bed."

"Who was giving you so much medication?"

"A close friend of my husband's," she said, "who just happens to be a psychiatrist. I've been planning to leave my husband for months, so I began weaning myself off the drugs, unbeknownst to my husband and my doctor. Which explains why I spiraled into mania," she added.

"What made you choose to come to Atlanta?"

"I contacted my old college roommate. She's an MD. She has been expecting me. I awoke this morning feeling clearheaded for the first time in days. I called her this morning; she has been frantic with worry and had tried to reach me at home, only to be told that I was ill and couldn't come to the phone," she added.

"Are you feeling suicidal, Elizabeth?" I asked.

"No. But I don't think my depression is all related to

my illness. I feel like crap for wasting ten years of my life with an abusive husband. He broke me down, Dr. Holly. I don't have to tell you what battered wife syndrome is like."

"He's the cause of those bruises on your arm?"

"Yes. I asked one of our employees to help me escape. I thought I could trust her. My mistake. I had to wait until the opportunity presented itself. I was already cycling into mania by that time, but I was able to pull myself together long enough to go to the bank and make a substantial withdrawal. I remember paying cash for a used car. I obviously went through the money quickly because I had to sleep in my car. I should never have stopped the medication I was taking for my bipolar illness, but I was so pissed off that I was being drugged. I don't want to be sedated anymore, Dr. Holly."

"You understand why Dr. Glazer was forced to give you something, right?" I asked. "You were experiencing serious mania at the time and, like you said, hallucinating. I can ask him to start cutting back on your Vistaril, but I think it's important that you remain on the mood stabilizer."

"I have no problem with that."

"I just have one more question," I said. "Why were you being drugged?"

"Have you ever heard of Tyler's Fine Foods?"

"You're *that* Tyler?"

"Sole owner and CEO," she said.

Which meant she was worth millions, I realized.

"I think my husband and my doctor hoped to prove me incompetent so my husband could have control of my assets."

It was a lot to take in. "This is all so remarkable," I said. Still, her thoughts and speech were logical and coherent. "Do you think your husband will try to find you?"

"Absolutely. Not only for my money but because he fears a scandal."

She lay back on the bed. I could see the extreme fatigue on her face. Tears glistened in her eyes. Telling me her story had taken a lot out of her.

"Elizabeth?" She looked at me. "I promise I will do everything in my power to protect you. I'm sure I speak for Dr. Glazer as well."

"Thank you." She closed her eyes.

I left the unit and walked to my car. I called Thad from my cell phone and told him what I'd learned. He was clearly stunned. "She doesn't want anyone to know who she is," I said. "I'm hoping she'll be stable enough to leave the hospital soon."

"Shouldn't Mrs. Larkin be talking to the police?" he said. "Or someone from a women's shelter?" he added.

"She has a safe place to go, Thad, and she appears to be in her right mind. I don't think she wants to involve the police."

"That's not the point," he said. "There are people trained to handle this sort of thing. You need to convince her to speak to them."

"I'll be in touch," I said, not wanting to hear a lecture.

My mom and aunt had packed the books in my office as well as my wall pictures and had gone out for a sandwich when Arnie Decker arrived with his father. Arnie was dressed in neat slacks and a dress shirt, minus sequins and polished fingernails. The man beside him was white haired but looked to be in perfect physical condition. His clothes were starched and creased. His face was tight.

Arnie fixed me with a look of sheer terror. "Dr. Holly, I'd like you to meet my father, Colonel Dean Decker."

"My pleasure, Dr. Holly," the man said, his voice as stiff as his clothes. His handshake was firm. "You may call me Colonel."

"I'm Kate," I said and motioned them toward my office. I invited them to be seated, but neither man made a move until I took my chair. "You'll have to excuse all the boxes," I said. "I'm in the process of moving to a new office."

"I'm clearly at a disadvantage," the colonel said. "I have absolutely no idea why I'm here. I did not even know Arnold was seeing a therapist."

Arnie squirmed. I didn't blame him for being uncomfortable. I was anxious as well.

"Thank you for coming, sir," I said. "I know it means a lot to your son."

"Shall we get started?" he said.

Arnie's gaze met mine before turning to his father. I nodded. "Well, sir, you know how important it was for me to serve my country."

"I should certainly hope so."

"I worked very hard to do the best job I could because I wanted you to be proud of me." He took a deep breath. "But it wasn't easy because I felt different from the rest of the men."

"Different? What do you mean?"

Arnie hesitated. Sweat beaded his brow. "I don't expect you to understand, sir, but I think I would have made a better daughter to you than a son."

The colonel frowned. "I haven't the first clue what you're talking about."

"I've never felt like a man, Father, and I've spent my entire life pretending to be something I'm not because I was afraid I would lose your respect. For as long as I can remember, I've felt like a female," he added.

"What the hell are you talking about?" the older man demanded.

I could see the red streaks creeping up the colonel's neck, even as he stared at his son in disbelief. He was clearly shaken.

"There's a term for it, Father. It's called gender identity disorder. I may look like a man on the outside, but the real me, the female side, has been trapped inside all these years. I want to start living my life as a woman."

"A woman!" the colonel bellowed. He looked at me. "Is this some kind of joke?"

His face was apple red; a sheen of sweat covered his brow. "No, sir," I said. "Gender identity disorder is very real. I've treated a number of patients who felt like, um, Arnold."

"You mean freaks, don't you?" he said, his voice booming. "People who belong in a circus," he added.

"Colonel, if we could just try to remain calm," I said, expecting Mona to knock on the door any moment to see if everything was okay.

He bolted to his feet, but I could see that he was unsteady.

"I refuse to listen to this garbage. Just thinking about it makes me sick to my stomach." He looked at Arnie. "A freak!" he repeated. "That's what you are."

I could see the anguish in Arnie's eyes as he stood and faced his father squarely. "I am *not* a freak!" he said sharply.

"Don't raise your voice to me," the colonel said.

Arnie hitched his chin a notch. "I am not asking for your approval, but I thought you should know that I'm going to start living full-time as a woman. I will eventually begin taking injections that will change my appearance and make me more feminine. In time, I'll have sexual reassignment surgery and become a real woman."

"This is going to kill your mother! After today you are no longer welcome in our home." He turned for the door.

I stood. Things had gone all wrong. "Colonel, please," I said. "Your son needs you to understand."

He whipped around. "My son?" he shouted. He pointed a finger at Arnie. "He is no son of mine."

Arnie stepped closer to the man. I could see the fury in his eyes. I hurried over and touched his shoulder, hoping to calm him, while at the same time prepared to back off in case they decided to slug it out.

"You're right, Father," he said between gritted teeth. "I'll be the daughter you never had."

The colonel threw open the door, but his whole demeanor changed, and he staggered out, and without warning, sank to his knees.

"Colonel!" I cried.

"Father!" Arnie was at the man's side in an instant, catching him before his head could hit the floor.

I looked at Mona. She was already calling for help.

"My pills!" the colonel gasped. "In my pants pocket."

Arnie and I both checked. I recognized the medication right away. I opened the bottle, dumped one of the tablets in my hand, and managed to slip it beneath his tongue. The colonel's eyes rolled back in his head, and I feared I might be too late. I began performing CPR on him as Arnie watched, tears streaming down his face.

"What's wrong with him?" Arnie cried.

"I think it's his heart," I said quickly, praying the ambulance would arrive soon.

"I didn't know he was ill," Arnie said.

The door to the reception room opened, and my mom and aunt stood there watching. "Holy h-e-l-l!" my mother said, thinking it was okay to curse as long as she spelled the words. "What's going on?"

"We think he might be having a heart attack," Mona said. "We're waiting for an ambulance."

"It's all my fault!" Arnie said, choking on his words. "I should never have told him I was going to become a woman."

My mother gaped. "You're going to become a woman?" she repeated. "Why would you do that?"

"You're such a handsome man," Aunt Trixie said.

"It's complicated," he managed between sobs.

I glanced up. "I need this room cleared so the paramedics can get a stretcher in here."

It seemed like forever before they arrived. I was sweat soaked and exhausted. My mother and aunt were trying to comfort Arnie as they stood just inside my office. I stepped aside to give the paramedics room to work.

"Please don't let him die," Arnie said to them. "I will never be able to live with myself."

"He's not going to die," my mother said. "This sort of thing happens on *General Hospital* all the time, and the patient almost never dies."

"She's right," Aunt Trixie said. "And when one of the patients actually does die, they bring him back."

Arnie swiped at his tears. Mona was wringing her hands. "I wish I were a real nurse."

"You need to be strong no matter what," my mother

told Arnie, "especially if you're thinking about becoming a woman. Women are a lot stronger than men."

The paramedics moved swiftly and efficiently. They checked the colonel's vital signs, gave him an injection, and hooked him to an IV. All the while, they exchanged information by radio. Finally, they lifted him on a stretcher and told us where they were taking him.

"I'll follow you in my car," Arnie said.

"You're in no condition to drive," my mother told him. "We'll take you in our truck."

"Thanks, Mom," I said as she and Aunt Trixie grabbed their purses to leave. "Please call me as soon as you learn anything."

Finally, Mona and I were alone. I sank into one of the chairs and buried my face in my hands.

"Are you okay?" Mona asked. "Would you like a Xanax?"

I shook my head. "This is all my fault. I should never have let things get so out of hand in there," I said, feeling worse by the minute.

"How were you supposed to know the man had a heart condition?" she said. "Besides, he's the one who went ballistic. I heard you trying to calm him down."

I was vaguely aware of Mona standing over me. "You're pale," she said. "I want you to lie down in your office. I'll let you know the minute I hear anything."

I allowed myself to be led to my sofa. Mona tucked a pillow beneath my head and covered me with a light throw. She reached behind a chair and pulled out the teddy bear we used with children, then tucked him beside me.

"What are you doing?" I said.

"You need to hold on to Bubba Bear," she said. "He always makes people feel better."

"I'm not a child!"

"It doesn't matter," she said. "Sometimes we just need something to hold on to." She yanked several tissues from the box on my coffee table. "Here."

I saw the earnest look on her face. Mona was doing all she knew to do to help. I took the tissues and mopped my eyes. "Thank you," I said.

"Now, I want you to close your eyes and do that meditation thing you do when you get stressed. I'll let you know the minute I hear something."

"I have patients."

"You're in no position to see them. I'm going to call them and tell them you had an emergency. It doesn't matter, anyway. They're way behind on their bills."

She closed the door, and I took several deep breaths. The good thing about being a hypnotist is knowing how to calm oneself through deep breathing and visualization. I imagined myself sitting on a beach watching a sunrise. I imagined the salty smell, the sun on my face, the breeze on my skin. I imagined everything being okay. Well, almost. If Arnie's father died, I would be partially to blame.

chapter 9

....

I must've fallen asleep, because when I opened my eyes, Jay and Mona were standing over me. I checked my wristwatch and discovered I'd been asleep for quite a while. "Are you okay, Katie?" Jay asked, leaning forward to stroke my cheek.

"What are you doing here?" I asked.

"I was really concerned about you," Mona said, "so I called him."

"But you're on duty," I said. "What will your men do without you?"

"Why don't you let me worry about that," he said.

I sat up. I realized I was holding Bubba Bear. "Have you heard from Arnie?" I asked Mona.

"Yes, and the colonel is going to be okay," she said. "I also rescheduled your patients."

"How is Arnie holding up?" I asked.

"He's good. Once he notified the rest of the family, your mother and aunt insisted he go home with them."

I shook my head. "Poor Arnie." But I knew my mom and aunt would take good care of him. They might clog his arteries with fried food and ask embarrassing questions about the surgical procedure that would make him a woman, but they'd pamper him and make him feel at home.

"Oh, and your mother said they'd be back tomorrow to finish packing."

The words had barely left her mouth before Mona seemed to realize her blunder. She slapped her hand over it, an apology in her eyes.

"I noticed all the boxes," Jay said. "What's going on?"

"We're, um, remodeling," Mona said before I could reply.

Jay shrugged it off and reached for my hand. "Let me drive you home, babe. You can even bring your teddy bear with you."

I blushed and handed Bubba Bear to Mona. I slipped my hand in Jay's, and he gently pulled me to my feet.

We took the elevator to the first floor and Jay led me to his SUV. "How about I stop on the way and pick up an order of waffles for you," he suggested. "That usually does the trick."

"I'm not very hungry," I said. I suddenly remembered Mike was at Lila's. I gave Jay directions to her place. We pulled into her driveway twenty minutes later.

"I'll walk you to the door," he said. "I want to see if this woman is for real."

Lila was clearly surprised to see us when she opened the door. "I wasn't expecting you until five thirty," she said. "I haven't even taken Mike and Prissy for their outing at the park."

"I wasn't feeling well so I left the office early," I said. I introduced her to Jay.

"Mike is in the den with my friend Claudia," Lila said. "Claudia is very good with animals that are experiencing a lot of distress. She uses a holistic approach."

Jay and I exchanged glances as we followed Lila to her den at the back of the house. She peeked inside the door and put her fingers to her lips. "Claudia is still working with Mike," she whispered.

I pushed the door open wider. I heard what sounded like a waterfall. I found Mike sprawled on what appeared to be a faux fur blanket on a sofa. Lighted candles sat on an end table. A young woman, dressed like she'd just stepped out of the sixties, lightly rubbed Mike's temples with her fingers. The woman looked up and gave a serene smile.

"What are you doing to my dog?" I asked.

In response, she raised a finger to her lips. She stood and crossed the room. She motioned for Jay and me to step into the hall. "Mike is in a state of deep relaxation," she whispered.

Again, Jay and I exchanged looks.

"Lila was so concerned about your poor little doggie that I came right away."

"What's wrong with Mike?" Jay asked.

Claudia shook her head sadly. "She's anxious and depressed. Have there been problems in the home?"

"No more than any other American home," I said defensively.

"The reason I ask," Claudia said, "is because I noticed how tight Mike's muscles were when I gave her a deep tissue massage."

I blinked dumbly. "You gave her a massage?"

"Yes, right after I gave her a special bath to open her pores. Her pores need to be able to breathe."

"I don't know why we didn't think of that," Jay said to me.

"I've been playing meditation music and using lavender and chamomile aromatherapy to help her relax. I think Mike is more sensitive than most canines. In fact, I believe she's highly attuned to everything that's going on around her." Claudia smiled. "I would encourage you to play soothing music and continue with the massages and aromatherapy on a daily basis for the next few weeks. I think you'll see a tremendous difference in your pooch."

"I'd like to take Mike home now," I said. I don't know why I was so annoyed except that everything looked and sounded wacky, and I knew Jay would have a good time with it at my expense.

"I'll wake her," Claudia said. She opened the door to the den and crossed the room. Jay and I watched from the doorway as she gently nudged Mike. Her eyelids fluttered, and she opened them. As if sensing someone else was in the room, Mike looked my way and wagged her tail. I walked over and lifted her. She was as limp as wilted lettuce, and her eyes were dazed.

"Ready to go home, girl?" I asked, still holding her. She wagged her tail again.

We followed Lila to the front of the house. "Let me grab Mike's treats from the kitchen," Lila said. She looked at Jay. "I call them Lila's love treats." She hurried away. I noted Prissy curled into a ball on the living room chair.

"I think Claudia hypnotized Mike," I said to Jay.

"I didn't know you could hypnotize animals." He stroked Mike's head. "She certainly seems relaxed."

Lila returned with the treats. I took the bag and thanked her, but I was anxious to leave.

"Be sure to let me know when you want to set up another playdate," Lila called out as Jay and I walked toward his SUV.

We'd barely pulled from Lila's driveway before Jay gave a grunt. "That's got to be the weirdest thing I've ever seen," he said. "I don't know, Katie. You seem to be a magnet for nutcases."

I leaned back in my seat. "So you've said."

"I'm not trying to be critical, babe, but you have to admit things were a little strange back there."

I didn't respond. I was glad when Jay pulled into my driveway. I climbed out and put Mike down. She seemed to stagger a bit before she got her footing. Jay followed me inside the house. Mike headed for her doggie door.

"Would you like to lie down?" Jay asked me. "You look wiped out."

"Actually, I'd like to grab a soda and sit in the backyard. I don't get outside much."

"Let's do it."

I grabbed two soft drinks from the refrigerator and unlocked my back door. Mike had obviously done her business, because she had found a patch of sun and stretched out on the lawn. Jay and I sat at a picnic table the previous tenants had left behind. The weather had worn the wood smooth.

"I love sitting out here," I said, opening my can and taking a sip.

Jay did the same. "You and I don't take enough time for relaxation, what with my work schedule, and the colorful situations you seem to find yourself in."

I didn't know if I was being overly sensitive, but his remark sounded like another dig. I wondered if he realized how critical he'd become.

"What do you know about gangs?" I asked, wanting to change the topic.

He arched one brow. "You thinking about joining one?"

I told him about the charges against Ricky, and the evidence that suggested he was guilty. "At first I thought the attack on the priest was gang related, but the evidence against Ricky is pretty damning."

"We see gang activity on a daily basis. It's becoming an epidemic, and not just in Atlanta." He took a sip of his drink. "They move in and claim a certain area, and it becomes their territory. If an opposing gang member is caught infringing on another's territory, it's a sure death sentence. They make their money on drugs and prostitution and extortion. Business owners are expected to pay for protection, and it doesn't come cheap."

"Sounds like the Mafia," I said.

"They're more dangerous than the Mafia, and there are more of them nationwide."

"Is it hard to tell one gang from another?"

"They have their own colors, tattoos, and hand signals. As in the case of the Crips and the Bloods, they wear their bandanas and their belt buckles differently in order to distinguish one from the other. The bad news is they're recruiting kids off the playground. There is an initiation. I don't know if you've ever heard of MS-13, but with that gang, an initiate is beaten by a number of members for thirteen seconds. That's a long time when you're getting kicked around by a violent group. Plus, once you're in, you're in for life."

"I just don't get it. Why would anyone attack an old priest?" I asked.

Jay looked thoughtful. "Maybe the priest was making trouble for the gang. Maybe he saw something. Who knows? Has he said anything?"

"He's in critical condition." I sighed. "Ricky is an honor student who has never been in trouble. He wants to go to medical school."

"Sometimes even the most promising kids cave in under pressure, Katie," he added. He looked at his soda and shook his head.

"What?"

"If this Ricky *is* part of a gang, then you're in way over your head. If the gang thinks he's talking, they'll go after him *and* you. They don't need much of a reason to kill," he added. "I don't know why you insist on getting involved with dangerous people."

I decided to change the subject. "I feel bad that I dragged you away from work," I said. "Especially with an arsonist on the loose," I added. "How is the investigation coming along?"

"The guy is smart as hell at covering his tracks. No fingerprints, no trace evidence, nothing. We're working with a special task force that compiles information from fire and police departments and other agencies, looking for the same MO. I think this guy has set fires before."

"Does anyone have an idea about motive?" I asked.

"You know the profile. It could be anything from anger, resentment, a feeling of inadequacy, sexual gratification—you name it. Of course, these people aren't as dangerous as the kind you're dealing with. They don't usually have an arsenal in the trunk of their car or get a thrill out of watching people die."

"I shouldn't have told you about Ricky."

"I'd like you to stop seeing him before you get in too deep."

"I can't do that," I said.

He looked annoyed. "What is it with you that you insist on getting involved in dangerous situations? Are you just looking for trouble?"

I felt a sudden, unexpected sting at the back of my eyes. The last thing I wanted to do was cry, but the day had taken a toll on me. I sat up straighter. "Since you're already unhappy with me, I should probably tell you what else is going on in my life."

"I'm almost afraid to hear it."

I took a deep breath and told him about the eviction, my attempt to find an affordable place, and, finally, agreeing to share Thad's office.

Jay didn't interrupt, but I watched the changing expressions on his face: surprise, disbelief, and, finally, anger.

He shook his head sadly but remained quiet.

"Aren't you going to say something?" I asked.

He shrugged. "What do you want me to say?" he asked. "That I'm hurt as hell that you didn't come to me in the beginning? That I feel like crap over the fact you chose to go to an old flame for help instead?" He gave a grunt. "That the two of you made arrangements to share his office without my knowledge?" he added. "This sort of takes our communication problems to a new level, don't you think?"

I felt a lone tear run down my cheek. "You know what else sucks?" I said. "You've done nothing but criticize me and make snide remarks about my profession and my patients for two months."

"I think I've had good reason."

"No," I said, my voice trembling. "There is never a good reason to make somebody feel small."

"Maybe one of the reasons it's so much easier for

you to talk to Thad is because he doesn't have as much at stake if something happens to you." He drained his soda and stood. "I have to get back to the station," he said.

I watched him walk away. I did not want him to leave, but I knew he would be in no mood to try and talk things through, and I was too weary to push.

Our relationship had hit a new low, and I felt powerless. I walked into the house and slumped on the sofa. The phone rang, and I hesitated before answering it. I didn't recognize the number on the caller ID; not even the area code.

I picked up and answered.

"Is Jay there?" a female voice asked.

"No, he's not," I said. "May I take a message?"

"This is Mandy Mason," the woman said. "You and I met at the station."

The probie with the big boobs, I thought.

"I've been trying to reach Jay on his cell phone, but he's not answering," she said. "Has he changed his number?"

He hadn't, but I didn't think it was any of her business. "Jay is on his way back to the station now."

"I'm sorry to have bothered you," she said. "I mean, Jay said the two of you were divorced, but I took a chance that he might be there. If you speak to him before I do, would you tell him I called?"

"Sure," I said, annoyed that Jay had shared our marital status with a woman that Mona and I both felt couldn't be trusted. It made me question whether I could trust Jay as well. I wondered where Mandy was calling from. "Should I tell Jay to call you at this number?"

"Yes, I'm in West Virginia." She hung up without another word. Although I wondered why Mandy was calling from such a distance away, I did not feel West Virginia was far enough.

My hands trembled as I added food to Mike's dish and gave her fresh water. It irked the hell out of me that Mandy had called me at home. Was she trying to tell me something? Had Jay given up on trying to work out our problems? That he'd walked out of our session with Evelyn and had just walked away from me weren't very good signs.

I tried to push it from my mind as I watched Mike gobble her food. I was surprised but happy that she had regained her appetite. Perhaps I had been too snippy with Lila and Claudia. Their tactics may have been strange, but they'd had Mike's best interests at heart, and they'd accomplished in an afternoon what I had not been able to do in weeks.

I pulled a frozen dinner from my freezer and popped it into the microwave, taking pride in the fact that I was able to get one meat, a carb, and a green vegetable for zero trans fats and less than three hundred calories. I saw that as progress, but when I sat down to eat I realized I had no desire for food. I needed to find something to occupy my time so I wouldn't dwell on the thought that Jay might be interested in another woman.

I turned on the radio and cleaned my house from top to bottom. I realized I was going to extremes when I found myself on my knees scrubbing the baseboards. But it was better than sitting around feeling sorry for myself, and the loud music kept me from thinking too much.

The goddess of hot water was with me as I ran a bubble bath and soaked for an hour. I shaved my legs, washed my hair, and exfoliated my face, which I seldom remembered to do even though Mona constantly reminded me how important it was. I gave myself a pedicure. By the time I left the bathroom, I felt like an old Buick sent in for a tune-up and oil change.

Wearing my nicest pajamas, I turned on the TV and searched for a decent movie, anything to occupy my mind. I hoped Arnie's father was okay; more than that, I hoped my mother was not driving poor Arnie up the wall.

I reminded myself, just as I'd reminded my patients time after time, that most of what we worried about was not within our control. Why was it so much easier to help others solve their problems, I wondered for the umpteenth time.

The next morning, I awoke feeling tired but happy that I had a clean house. I trudged downstairs in search of caffeine. I had just filled my mug when the phone rang. I prayed it was Jay, but the caller ID informed me it was my mother. I picked up.

"Have you seen the morning news?" she asked.

"I just woke up," I said. "Why?"

"Firefighters responded to a four-alarm fire at about five a.m. Jay's engine company was involved."

"Thanks." I hung up, carried my coffee to the living room, and turned to the local news. A reporter was speaking from a microphone.

"To recap the story," he said, "two search and rescue workers were injured when a floor collapsed beneath them as they entered a burning building in south-side Atlanta at dawn. The six-story apartment building had been boarded up and scheduled for demolition, but a neighbor reported seeing people come and go at odd hours. A body was carried from the burning structure; the victim appears to have been a homeless person, but details are sketchy at the moment.

"Firefighters evacuated an apartment building next door, worried the blaze might spread. Those who watched the blaze said they were amazed how quickly the flames engulfed the building."

"That's because it's arson, you idiot," I said to the TV.

"We're still waiting for word on those injured fire-fighters," the reporter added.

The camera panned out. Fire trucks and rescue vehicles were parked in front of what was left of the building, a charred and smoking skeleton. I looked for Jay in the crowd but didn't see him. I sent up prayers that he was okay. Then I sent up prayers that the other guys were okay.

I was still sitting in front of the TV when my phone rang. I raced to it. Jay spoke from the other end. "I wanted to let you know I'm okay."

Relief flooded me. "It's the same guy, isn't it?" I said.

He hesitated. "Yeah."

"By the way, Mandy called here yesterday, said she was in West Virginia. She wants you to call her back." I paused. "Frankly, I'm surprised you gave her my phone number and told her we're divorced."

He was quiet for a moment. "And I'm surprised you'd think I did that."

The next thing I heard was a dial tone.

I called my mother. I knew she would be concerned about Jay. "I just heard from Jay," I said. "He's fine." I heard her sigh of relief. I wondered if she was thinking of my father. "So how is Arnie?" I asked.

"We're really enjoying having him here," she said. "He had someone fill in for him at work last night, and he cooked beef Wellington for us. The secret to gourmet cooking is how much booze you put into it," she said.

"I didn't know," I said. "No wonder everything I cook tastes like crap."

"Arnell has decided to stay through the weekend and teach me how to cook some of his prizewinning recipes. And he is so impressed with our junk art."

"Everyone is," I said. "Why do you think decorators are willing to pay so much for it?"

"What a nice thing to say, Kate. Trixie and I will be in around nine."

I hung up. It occurred to me that I hadn't heard Mike get up and head out her doggie door. I walked into the laundry room and turned on the light. She looked dead to the world. "Get up you lazy, good-for-nothing dog," I called out cheerfully. She didn't budge. I walked over to her box and nudged her with my toe. No movement.

Fear hit me like a brick. "Mike, wake up!" I said loudly, reaching over to shake her. I took solace in the fact that her body was warm and she was breathing. I tried shaking her again. I noticed the plastic bag that had contained Lila's love treats lying beside her. Only a handful remained. I suddenly remembered I'd left the bag on the coffee table. Mike must've seen them and carried the bag to her bed.

I almost tripped over my own feet as I raced to the phone and dialed Jeff's number. He answered on the first ring. "Something's wrong with Mike!" I cried. "I can't wake her."

"Is she breathing?" he asked quickly.

"Yes, but she's not responding."

"Could she have gotten into something outside? Like a pesticide or—"

"I don't see how," I said. "My backyard is fenced." I started to cry.

"I'm on my way to the office now," he said. "How soon can you be there?"

"Ten minutes max," I said, praying I wouldn't be slowed by traffic.

I hung up. I raced upstairs, exchanged my PJs for sweats, and shoved my feet into old loafers. Back on the main floor, I grabbed my purse, scooped Mike gently from her bed, and panicked when I found her limp. I scanned the room to see if there was anything she could have gotten into, but all my cleaning supplies were stacked on a shelf above the washer and dryer. I snatched the plastic bag of treats and stuffed it in my purse before running out the door.

Jeff was standing just outside his office building when I pulled up. He carried Mike from my car to his exam room and shined a light in her eyes as his technician drew blood.

"I'm giving her vitamin K, which should help in case she has ingested something," he said. "Dogs will eat anything."

I nibbled my bottom lip. "I thought she was acting funny yesterday," I said.

"Funny how?" he asked.

"She was sort of staggering." I told Jeff what I'd found when I arrived to pick Mike up from her play-date. "I should have brought her in right then," I said, feeling guilty, "but there was a lot going on at the time."

"Did this Claudia person mention giving Mike anything from her holistic medicine bag?" he asked.

"No. The only thing I've fed Mike is the food I purchased here and the dog treats Lila gave me. She calls them Lila's love treats." I pulled the plastic bag from my purse. "The bag was full when I went to bed last night. As you can see, Mike pigged out. Maybe she ate too much and it made her sick."

Jeff opened the bag and took a whiff. He frowned, pulled out a dog treat, and broke it in half. He sniffed it. Finally, he held the bag to the light. "Damn, Kate, I think these treats contain pot."

I felt my jaw drop. "You mean marijuana?" I asked. "How on earth can you tell?"

"My older brother used to bake brownies made with pot. I remember the smell." He pointed. "Look, there are even a few seeds at the bottom of the bag."

I just looked at him. "You're saying Mike—"

"I'm saying your dog is stoned."

chapter 10

I was seething with fury by the time I left Jeff's office. The blood test had confirmed his suspicion. Luckily, by the time I left, Mike was beginning to come around, but Jeff planned to keep her all day for observation. He assured me she would be okay after she'd slept for a while.

I drove straight to Lila Higginbothom's house and pounded on her door. She answered it wearing a bathrobe and pink sponge curlers. I put my finger in her face. "I know what you put in your so-called love treats," I said. "Mike is detoxing at the vet's office right now."

"Oh dear!" Lila said, the color draining from her cheeks. "I knew I shouldn't have listened to Claudia, but Prissy wasn't eating at the time, and Claudia convinced me that a little marijuana would help with her appetite." She paused and sucked in air. "I was so concerned about poor Mike that I doubled the amount in the last batch."

I shot her my most menacing look. "You had no right!" I yelled. "I trusted you to take good care of her. I thought you were a nice old lady," I added through gritted teeth.

"I *am* a nice old lady!"

"I should call the cops and have you busted," I said. "Do you have any idea what they do to nice old ladies in prison?"

Her eyes widened in fright. "No, what?"

"I have no idea, but I'm sure it can't be good."

Her hands flew to her chest and she sagged against the door. "Oh dear!" she cried.

I reached for her. "You'd better *not* be having a heart attack!"

"No, I just tinkled in my Depends."

"Don't ever come near me again," I said. "And don't ever come near my dog." I whirled around and headed to my car.

"Please don't rat me out to the fuzz," she called out. "I'm going to flush the marijuana down the toilet right now."

I raced home, took a five-minute shower, and dressed quickly. I brushed my lashes with mascara, ran a blusher across my cheeks, and pulled my hair into a ponytail. I arrived at the office in record time and found Mona sitting at the kitchen table in the back sipping a cup of coffee. I was surprised she wasn't wearing her nurse uniform but didn't mention it. Instead, I told her about Mike and Lila Higginbothom, as well as Jay's reaction once I'd told him about the eviction and my decision to share an office with Thad.

"You'd think he would at least be pleased that it's a great career opportunity," she said. "In the meantime, I would call the cops and report that old bag, Lila, for giving Mike pot."

"I don't think she'll do it again. I think I scared the hell out of her." I poured a cup of coffee and joined Mona at the table. "By the way, Mandy called me looking for Jay."

"What the hell did *she* want? And why did she call your house?"

I shrugged. "Your guess is as good as mine."

"I don't trust that bitch for one minute."

I was surprised at Mona's harsh tone and wondered if it had to do with her distrust of Liam. I said nothing.

"Did you tell Jay about the call?"

"Yeah. The conversation was short but not so sweet."

"I hate men," she said. "Which is why I've decided to break it off with Liam," she added.

"What happened?"

"I'm pretty sure he's cheating on me."

"I find that hard to believe, Mona. He's crazy about you."

"Or so he says," she snapped. "He denies having an affair, but I know the signs to look for. I read *Cosmo*."

"What did he do to make you so suspicious?"

"Like I said, he's exhausted all the time. He's too tired for sex, even when I wear my leather outfit. And he is forever canceling dates with me."

"He's a medical student doing his internship, for Pete's sake," I reminded her. "Of course he's tired."

"We'll see about that," she said. "I hired a private investigator. Last night while Liam was at the hospital, the investigator attached a live GPS beneath his car. I'll know where he is at all times."

I pressed the ball of my hand against my forehead. "I can't believe you did that."

"I refuse to let him make a fool of me." Her cell phone rang. She glanced at the number and ignored it.

"Is that Liam?"

"Who else? He's been calling every hour on the hour. He probably knows I suspect something."

"I've never seen you like this," I said. "Is it because he's younger than you?"

"I don't want to talk about it. But I've decided not to go to nursing school after all."

"What about your calling? I thought you wanted some kind of purpose."

"I'll find a different cause, but I have no desire to empty bedpans, and I can't stand the sight of blood."

She shuddered. "No man is worth putting myself through that."

My mom and Trixie arrived just as my young ADHD patient and his mother showed up. We spent the next hour going over his progress charts. His teachers, who'd been ready to pull their hair out over his unruly behavior in the beginning, had been so impressed over the changes they'd seen that I'd received a couple of referrals from the school's guidance counselor.

I gave myself an imaginary pat on the back as I walked them out. It never failed. Just when I thought I should throw in the towel and find a new career, one of my patients had a breakthrough or a small success and I felt good that I had played a part in it.

I found my mom and aunt finishing up the last of the packing in my supply room. "Is there any news on Arnie's father?" I asked.

"He's better," my mother said. "I guess doctors can repair a person's heart easily enough, but they can't fill it with love."

"Oh, that just gave me goose pimples," Mona said, rubbing her arms briskly.

My mother looked smug. "I can be deep like that."

"Any calls?" I asked Mona, hoping one of them might be from Jay.

"You had a call from a Dr. James Hudson," she told me, handing me my phone messages. "He said it was urgent that he see you today. I scheduled him to come in right after Alice Smithers."

I didn't recognize the name. "Did he say what it was about?"

"Nope. Only that it was of the utmost importance."

My mother looked eager. "Did you purchase a lottery ticket or respond to an online survey?"

I shook my head.

"I'll bet I know what it's about," Trixie said. "The bowling alley was raffling off a beautiful red bowling ball, and I filled out a card for everyone. I'll bet you won!"

I looked from my mother to my aunt and wondered what it must feel like to live in their world. Then, noting their lively expressions, I decided it must be pretty fantastic.

Alice Smithers showed up at noon, prompt as usual. I was surprised to find her wearing makeup, fashionable eyeglasses, and an attractive business suit. I wondered if Emily had been in charge of choosing the outfit. I knew Liz Jones had not selected it; it was far too tame.

"You look very nice today," I said.

She smiled. "Remember the guy I mentioned who works in purchasing and has been so nice to me?"

I had vague memories of the conversation. With Alice I was so accustomed to dealing with alter personalities that I was thrown off guard when we discussed someone who didn't actually live in her head. "What about him?" I asked.

"He asked me out."

"What did you say?"

Alice gave me an odd look. "I can't *possibly* go out with him," she said, "so I told him I was already involved with someone. I really like him, which is why I spent half the night crying."

"What are you afraid of?"

"You have to ask? What if he met Liz and figured he could get laid?"

"You just said he was a nice guy," I told her. "Liz isn't exactly into nice guys, and she would be bored in an accounting office."

"I can't take the chance. I'm sort of down in the dumps about it," she said. "I've always dreamed of getting married and having a family, but what man would want to get involved with someone like me? And who could blame him?"

"You're getting better every day, Alice." She didn't look convinced. "How have your sessions with Dr. Glazer been going?"

"I'm not usually present for those. I think that's when Liz chooses to come out. If that's the case, Lord only knows what he thinks of me."

I already knew that Liz was the major personality in the sessions with Thad. I also knew she didn't wear underwear because Thad complained about it constantly. Under any other circumstances, he would have loved it, but he didn't appreciate it in his patients, and he'd told Liz to clean up her act or else. Whatever that meant.

"Dr. Glazer wouldn't judge you because of Liz's behavior."

Again, Alice looked doubtful.

"Would you mind if I spoke with Sue?" I asked. "She can probably give me more information as to what's been going on with the others."

Alice shrugged. "Sure." She went still for a few seconds, and I noted the subtle changes that took place in her demeanor. Since Sue had 20/20 vision, she removed the eyeglasses. I was about to speak to her when, suddenly, I saw another change. The person on the sofa slumped and leaned forward, elbows on knees.

"Sue?" I asked.

"I'm not Sue," a voice said.

It was a male voice.

I tried not to act surprised, even though he'd caught me off guard. "I don't believe we've met," I said evenly.

"I know who *you* are," he told me.

He had a Southern twang. "Would you mind introducing yourself?" I asked.

"Alice used to call me Alley Cat," he said.

"That's an unusual nickname."

"I kilt cockroaches for her. That was a long time

148

back. We were just young'uns. I use to call her Scaredy Cat because she was scart of creepy crawlin' thangs."

His accent was hard to understand. "So, you've been around for a while," I said. "Why have we never met?"

He shrugged. "I ain't felt much like talkin'."

"I haven't seen any entries from you in the journal, either," I added.

"I ain't felt like writin'. Besides, I ain't a good speller."

"How old were you when you met Alice?" I asked.

"We were both five years old. When Alice got really scart, I helped out. She probably don't 'member. You ask me, at's a good thang."

"What made her so afraid?"

"That bitch mother of hers. 'At woman was a good-fer-nuthin' drunk. Always whorin' around. She did a lot of waitress work at truck stops 'cause she had a thang for truckers. She'd do okay fer a while, then she'd lay out drunk fer a few days, get fired, and we'd move on. Always lived on the run, you know? Lived in a lot of dumps," he added. "Like white trash."

I dreaded what I might hear next. "Did any of the truck drivers hurt Alice?"

"Naw, it was that bitch Carmen. The mother," he added. "She had unusual punishments if Alice didn't do 'xactly as she was told. Like lock her in a closet."

I listened, but I had to be careful about getting too close to the pictures in my head. Nobody wants to think about a young child being abused, not even me, and that's my job.

He crossed his arms. "Only sometimes Carmen'd get drunk and ferget Alice was in there. Like fer a couple of days. Alice tried so hard not to pee her britches, you know, 'cause Carmen would go into a fit. She hit Alice lots. I would'a kilt Carmen if I could have," he added bitterly.

"But you were only five years old," I reminded him gently. "Children should not have to defend themselves from their parents. Alice was lucky to have someone in there with her," I said. "You've been with her ever since?"

"We growed up together, but I don't come 'round much now that Carmen is outta the picture." He looked me square in the eye. "That's 'bout all I gots to say, but I thought you should know."

And then he was gone.

Dr. James Hudson was waiting in the reception room as I led Alice out. He looked to be in his early sixties. He had thinning gray hair, slightly bulging eyes, and was impeccably dressed in a suit that was of the same caliber as the ones Thad wore. I led him inside my office, invited him to sit on my sofa, and took the chair beside him. He looked around. I could tell he was not impressed. "You'll have to excuse all the boxes," I said. "I'm in the process of moving."

"I can't say I blame you," he replied.

I thought the remark rude, but I ignored it. "How may I help you?" I asked, using my Dr. Laura Schlessinger voice.

He handed me his business card. "I'm a practicing psychiatrist, licensed in the state of Vermont. I'm here on behalf of a patient. Your colleague, Dr. Thad Glazer, admitted her to the psychiatric unit a few days ago. She was using the name Marie Osmond."

"Oh?" I said, trying to remain professional, which meant it was unethical for me to tell him Thad and I were treating a patient or even knew the person. At the same time, I felt contempt for the man. He had been responsible for drugging Elizabeth Larkin and stealing a large chunk of her life.

"I attempted to reach Dr. Glazer this morning," he went on, "but I understand he is on the golf course and isn't answering his cell phone. Frankly, I find that disconcerting."

I gave him a benign smile. "He turns his phone off on the golf course because he's afraid it will ring while he's teeing off."

Hudson said nothing. He seemed to look through me as if I had no real importance in the world.

"I'm sure Dr. Glazer will get back to you soon," I said.

"I don't have time to wait until he finishes eighteen holes of golf. I'm deeply concerned about my patient."

"I'm sure I don't have to remind you of confidentiality laws, Dr. Hudson," I said stiffly.

His smile was condescending. "I came prepared,"

he said, pulling an envelope from a pocket inside his jacket. "I retained legal counsel in this state shortly after my arrival yesterday. You'll note we've already been before a judge. I have a court order releasing Mrs. Larkin into my custody."

I looked through the paperwork. He had not overlooked anything. "I'm impressed," I said. "Imagine being able to accomplish all this without first consulting with Dr. Glazer or myself."

He gave an impatient wave of his hand. "I'm a busy man, and this is a highly sensitive matter, Dr. Holly."

"What if Mrs. Larkin doesn't wish to go back with you?"

"She has not been well for some time now," he said, "which is why the judge agreed to hand her over to me."

"That, and the fact that she's married to somebody important," I said. Again, no response, but I could tell he didn't like it. We were not bonding. "How did you know where to find her?"

"We've had people looking for her since her disappearance more than a week ago."

I wondered what her important husband would make of his wife's new country western outfits. I handed Dr. Hudson his sheath of legal forms. "You obviously have all you need to take her back. Why are you here?"

"I don't know her present state of mind," he said. "I was hoping you could enlighten me. It's in everyone's best interest if we avoid a scene." He paused. "I don't know if you or Dr. Glazer picked up on it, but Mrs. Larkin is bipolar."

He acted as though he expected me to be surprised. "Oh yes," I said. "Dr. Glazer and I pretty much figured it out when we went coon hunting the other night."

"Why the sarcasm, Dr. Holly? Surely you know I have my patient's best interests at heart."

I leaned back in my chair. "Frankly, I don't appreciate your going behind my back so you can yank a seriously depressed woman out of the hospital," I said. "Where is her husband, by the way? Why did he not personally come for his wife?"

"Again, it's a sensitive matter. He does not want his wife's picture plastered on the front page of every newspaper in the country. As for her emotional health, I think I would be the better judge. You've been treating her for what, three days?"

Again, that condescending smile. I decided to try and wipe it off his face. "Then you're aware that her husband was physically abusing her."

"That's preposterous!"

"She carries the bruises, Dr. Hudson."

"Did she *say* she'd been abused?"

"She was experiencing a manic break when I first saw her, so she wasn't able to give us much information. A good beating could have caused a break."

"You're out of line, doctor," he said, his face turning dark. "Elizabeth stopped taking her medication. That would easily have caused her to cycle into mania."

I buzzed Mona, and she picked up. "Would you please call Dr. Glazer and ask him to get back to me as soon as possible. Try to reach him on his cell phone."

"I'm on it," Mona said.

I sat back in my chair. "Dr. Glazer ordered extensive blood work once Mrs. Larkin was admitted to the hospital," I said. "She had enough drugs in her system to bring a hippopotamus to its knees."

"I resent that remark," he said. "Not only is it wrong, it's unprofessional." He scooted forward in his chair. "I don't know how *you all* do things down here, but—"

"We're simple people, Dr. Hudson," I interrupted. I was so pissed that I wished I could throw something at him, but everything was packed. "If we have a difference of professional opinion, we usually get liquored up and arm wrestle. If we can't settle it the civilized way, we have a spitting contest."

His face turned red, and the anger in his eyes was scalding. I wondered if Elizabeth had seen that look and been afraid not to follow his instructions. Bad enough that her husband had been abusive; her doctor was equally so but in a different way.

"The law is clearly on my side," he said. "I have the legal right to take her back with me, with or without your cooperation."

Mona buzzed me. "Thad's on the line," she said when I answered.

I picked up. "I have a situation, Dr. Glazer," I said formally and went on to explain what was happening.

154

Thad wasted no time. "Dr. Hudson has a legal right to take his patient back with him."

"It's a bad idea," I said, remembering my promise to Elizabeth that I would protect her.

"As I see it you have two choices, Kate," he said. "You can adhere to the judge's orders or be held in contempt. Not only could you be fined, you might spend a few days in jail."

"You and I need to discuss this further, Thad."

"There is nothing to discuss," he said. "The bottom line is, I don't want to get caught up in a messy situation. You need to cooperate with Mrs. Larkin's doctor."

I hung up on him. I grabbed my purse from the bottom drawer of my desk and smiled at Dr. Hudson. "If you're ready, I'll drive you to the hospital."

He returned my smile. "I'm glad Dr. Glazer was able to talk some sense into you."

I felt like punching him. He followed me out. "By the way, do you like chili dogs?" I asked. "This hospital has the best chili dogs in the world."

"Dr. Holly—"

"You probably don't eat many chili dogs where you come from. Just syrup."

Edith Wright greeted us. She took one look at my face, and I saw her body go stiff, meaning she knew something was up. Edith could be quick like that. "I

155

received the faxes from the attorney's office, Dr. Hudson," she said, showing no emotion.

"How is her depression?" I asked and noted that my question drew a frown from Dr. Hudson.

"We didn't have to put her on suicide watch after all," she said.

"Suicide watch?" Hudson gave a grunt of disgust. "I assure you, my patient is not suicidal. This is precisely how nasty rumors get started. This is how hospitals find themselves in the midst of a lawsuit."

Edith rewarded him with a dark look. "Go ahead and make my day," she said.

I wanted to applaud her.

"I'd like to see my patient now, if you don't mind," he said stiffly.

Edith smiled at me. "How about I have Big Debra escort you to the dayroom in case the patient gets out of hand."

I returned her smile. "How awfully nice of you, Nurse Wright," I said, as she sauntered behind the nurses' station and picked up the phone.

Debra appeared wearing her most menacing frown. Dr. Hudson did a double take. She towered over him and was twice his width. "This way," she ordered.

I leaned close to Hudson. "Do what she says," I told him. "You don't want to make her angry."

He dutifully followed her with me on his heels.

Elizabeth was sitting alone near the window in the dayroom. Debra stopped just inside the door and crossed her arms.

Elizabeth looked up. She was clearly not pleased to see her doctor. That in itself convinced me she was on the mend. "What are you doing here?"

"Did you not think we would look for you, dear?" Hudson said. "Your husband is distraught." He winced. "What on earth have you done to your hair?"

Elizabeth patted both sides. "You don't like it?" she asked, looking upset. "Oh my, you must think I'm crazy!" She covered her mouth, and her eyes rolled about like marbles gone haywire.

I had to look away. Even Debra seemed amused. I would now be able to tell people I was present the day Debra smiled.

"We'll have you all fixed up before John returns from Washington," Hudson said, showing frown lines. He was not having fun. "Your private jet is waiting to take you home."

I touched Elizabeth's shoulder. Our gazes met. "Are you feeling less confused than you were this morning?" I asked.

"Well, I—" She paused. "I still sometimes think I can fly."

Hudson appeared shocked. "Fly?"

Debra gave a grunt. "She would have flown right out of these windows if they didn't have bars on them."

Elizabeth nodded. "And I get so scared in the hallway. I keep seeing lions and tigers and bears."

I gasped. "Lions and tigers and bears? Oh my!"

Hudson looked bewildered.

"Do you need anything from your room before you go?" I asked.

"I don't know which room is mine."

"Would you like me to help you get your things together?" I asked. "I know you're anxious to be on your way."

"That's very kind of you, Dr. Holly," she said.

I looked at Hudson. He was about to burst out of his skin with impatience. "It won't take long."

"I'll keep him company," Debra said, in a voice that sounded as though she'd prefer cleaning toilets.

We left the room. "I'm going to try and get you out of here," I said in a low voice, "but we don't have much time. What do you need from your room?"

"Just my purse."

I waited outside her door while she hurried in and grabbed it. "This way," I said, nodding toward the hall. "Now, I need you to listen carefully."

"I'm all ears."

"As soon as I get back to my office, I'm going to call a friend of mine who is a psychiatrist. I'm sure I can get you in tomorrow morning, which is when you're due to take the next dose of your medication. You *can't* stop taking your medication, Elizabeth. You could start cycling again."

She nodded. "Okay."

"Do you have your friend's address and phone number?"

"In my pocketbook," she said. "I also have the key to her house in case she's not home."

"I want you to call me as soon as you get there so I can give you this doctor's name and the time of your appointment." I reached inside my purse for a business card. "Can you remember to do that?"

"Yes."

"I need to know that you're okay, Elizabeth," I said sternly. "Do not forget to call me."

"I promise."

I smiled and nodded calmly at the hospital staff as I led Elizabeth toward the back of the unit. To most people it would appear as if we were simply taking a stroll.

We had reached our destination; the freight elevator was only a few feet away. The short hall was clear. I used my key to access the elevator and punched the "down" button. We waited.

"I hope you made your husband sign a prenup," I said.

"Of course I did. I may be crazy, but I'm not stupid."

"Will he try to come after you?"

"Once he realizes I'm in my right frame of mind, he and Dr. Hudson will most likely tuck their tails and run. As soon as I'm back to my old self I'll call a lawyer."

"Make certain that your friend gets pictures of your bruises."

"Of course."

The elevator door slid open. Noting that the hallway was still clear, I held the door in place with my foot and motioned Elizabeth inside.

She reached for my hand. "I'll never forget you for helping me," she said.

I squeezed her hand gently. "Okay, you're going to take this elevator to the basement where the morgue is located."

She swallowed. "The morgue?"

"It's the only way I can get you out of here without being seen. Once you get off the elevator, ask for Skeeter."

"Skeeter," she repeated.

"Tell him I sent you and that he is to drive you to your friend's house. You can trust him."

She nibbled her bottom lip. "Will I see dead bodies down there?"

"Not if you don't look. But Skeeter may have to smuggle you out in a hearse." I let go of her hand and stepped back. The elevator door closed.

I turned and my heart almost leapt from my chest as I found a woman with unruly hair and a dazed look standing in the hall, watching. "Did you see anything?" I asked.

"I'm waiting for my bus," she said. "Do you know if it stops here?"

I found Edith at the nurses' station. "I can't find my patient," I said. "I've searched the entire unit, but there is no sign of her."

Edith didn't look up from the form she was filling out. "Don't share."

"It's likely to get ugly."

She looked at me. "You know I don't like ugly," she said. "Especially from snobby psychiatrists."

"If he makes trouble, threaten to call the police. Trust me, he does not want them involved."

"Don't you have someplace you need to be, doctor?" she asked. Edith hit the buzzer, and I walked through the metal doors and out of the unit.

chapter 11

· ·

I made my way straight to the elevators and punched the button. Despite the adrenaline flooding through my veins and making me shaky all over, I was relieved that I'd managed to help Elizabeth Larkin escape what must've been a dismal and frightening existence. Although I felt guilty for leaving Edith to contend with Hudson, I knew she could handle him. I almost pitied the man.

The elevator came to a stop, and the doors slid open. Carter Atkins stood inside.

"Going down, Kate?" he asked.

Of all times to run into him, I thought. I was glad to see two businessmen standing at the back, briefcases in hand, chatting quietly. I don't know why I felt uneasy around Carter. It wasn't like I didn't deal with weird people on a daily basis.

"Hello, Carter," I said, stepping inside the elevator. The doors closed and we started down.

"I see you're visiting the folks on the third floor," he said, his voice barely above a whisper. "I try to avoid that floor."

"It's not so bad," I said, even though I had no desire to be there at the moment.

"Hey, did you hear Jay got rid of the sex kitten at work?" he asked.

I figured it was best to play dumb. "What happened?"

"Let me see if I can put this kindly," he said.

"Don't bother on my account."

"She didn't fit in. She wanted, um, preferential treatment." He leaned closer. "You ask me, she's got problems. I figure that's why her old man asked Jay to help her get the job."

I nodded. It explained why Mandy's call had come from West Virginia, but it didn't explain why she had been trying to reach Jay.

"How is the new guy doing? Ronnie Sumner," I added.

"Everybody thinks he's the best thing since inside plumbing," he said. "He can do no wrong. You ask me, he's too good to be true, you know?"

"What do you mean?"

Carter cut his eyes toward the businessmen and said nothing until the elevator stopped and we stepped outside. "Don't you think it's a little suspicious that the arsons started about the same time Sumner came to work?" he asked.

I glanced around; no sign of Hudson. "What are you saying?"

"Who would know better than another firefighter how to booby trap a building so that other firefighters would get hurt or killed?"

"Carter, what the hell are you talking about?"

"Don't you know?" he asked. "The arsonist is targeting firefighters."

I felt my head spin. Carter took my arm and pulled me aside. "Why do you think so many firefighters are landing in the hospital?" he said. "The arsonist plans what building he's going to torch; then, he does things like cut holes in the floors and covers them with vinyl or carpet, and the firefighters fall through. Last week several guys were trying to get a hose up a flight of stairs and it gave out because the person setting the fires had gone in ahead of time and sawed off some of the boards underneath."

I couldn't believe what I was hearing. Why hadn't Jay told me? I suddenly remembered there was probably a bad-ass psychiatrist looking for me. "I have to go," I said, starting for the double glass doors leading out.

Carter followed. "And get this," he said. "Sumner told everyone he was divorced. He lied. His wife died in a house fire. *Their* house," he added. "Why would he lie about something like that?"

"How do you know all this?" I said once we cleared the building.

"I asked a friend to do some checking on the Internet once it became obvious that the arsonist was so knowledgeable."

"But the news media—"

"It's all hush-hush right now."

I glanced over my shoulder.

"Are you trying to avoid someone?" Carter asked.

"It's a long story." I spotted my car a short distance away. Carter followed me to it. I fumbled in my purse for my keys. "How many suspicious fires have there been?" I asked.

"Not that many. I guess it takes him time to find a building and rig it. He uses an accelerant that doesn't burn black smoke or leave an odor, which would indicate that something wasn't right. A firefighter would know that sort of thing. But when a building is blazing out of control, you can barely see your hand in front of your face, so nobody knows the place is booby-trapped until it's too late."

I was shaken by the news. I felt sick to my stomach. "Did you tell Jay your suspicions about Sumner?"

Carter looked embarrassed. "I've been banned," he said. "I got caught going through Sumner's locker. I was looking for evidence."

"What!"

"Yeah," he said, looking sad and disappointed. "Jay said he would press charges if I ever set foot near the place again," he added.

"I have to go, Carter," I said, afraid my luck was about to run out where Hudson was concerned. I slid into the front seat of my car and reached for the door handle.

"You need to tell Jay," he said.

I nodded. I started my car and backed out. I was forced to stop and wait for another car to pull from one of the parking slots. "Come on!" I said, tapping my fingers on the steering wheel and glancing toward the entrance to the hospital. My head buzzed from everything that Carter had told me, and I suddenly felt panicky about helping Elizabeth escape. I wondered how much trouble I was in.

I reached the main road just as the light turned red. I cursed my bad luck. But then I saw something that lifted my dark mood. A hearse rounded the hospital and followed the road leading to one of the exits. I caught a split-second look at Skeeter's profile before he turned and headed in the opposite direction.

I was in panic mode by the time I reached my office. I had counted every stoplight on the way.

"Where have you been and why haven't you returned my calls?" Mona said as I stepped inside the reception room. "I had to cancel one of your appointments."

"Sorry," I said. "I had to turn off my cell phone in the hospital, and I forgot to turn it back on." I figured that by the time things settled down I wouldn't have any patients left.

"Thad is in your office, and he is not happy."

"Wow, that was fast." He'd obviously gotten a call from Hudson the minute the man had realized Elizabeth was missing.

"And your uncle Bump called and asked that you call him back as soon as possible." She paused. "Boy, you look like hell. Do you want a Xanax?"

"No, I'd rather just white-knuckle my way through the rest of the day. Where are my mom and Trixie?"

"You just missed them. Everything is packed and ready to go."

"I need you to make a few calls for me," I said. "First, try to contact Jay. I *have* to talk to him. You've got his cell number, right?" Mona nodded. "Then contact Delores Spears."

"The psychiatrist?"

"Yes. Tell her I've referred a patient, and it's urgent that she see her first thing in the morning. If she has questions, put her through to me right away."

"Okay."

"When Elizabeth calls, give her the information, including Delores's phone number and address. And make sure she's safe."

"Are you going to tell me what's going on?"

"Trust me. The less you know, the better." I started for my office. "Oh, one more thing. Call Jeff Henry and find out how Mike is doing."

"I'm on it," Mona said.

I entered my office and found Thad reclining on my sofa. He began clapping at the sight of me. "Way to go,

Kate!" he said. "Security guards are scouring hospital grounds as we speak because, as unbelievable and archaic as it sounds, a mental patient has escaped from the psychiatric ward. Dr. Hudson assured me that Senator Larkin will have our licenses over this."

"He's full of hot air," I muttered, sitting at my desk.

"I'm not finished," Thad said. "Edith punched Hudson in the face and broke his nose."

"I knew she would do me proud."

Thad got up from the sofa and placed both hands on my desk. He looked directly into my eyes. "It's okay if you want to ignore court orders and screw with your own professional career, Kate," he said, "but it's not okay to take me down with you."

"Okay, Thad, listen up. Larkin is not going to do a damn thing to us because his wife will mop the floors of hell with him if he makes trouble. He has been physically and emotionally abusing her. Why do you think Hudson was keeping her drugged? So she wouldn't tell," I said. "Senator Larkin can't afford more bad press."

"Gee, I hope you're right for once."

I frowned. "What's that supposed to mean?"

"You don't always make wise decisions, Kate."

I'd had enough crap for one day. "You know what, Thad? Not only do I not like you very much right now, I don't even want to talk to you. And I damn sure don't want to share office space with you."

He looked surprised. Shocked, actually, I thought. I decided I liked that look on him.

"You're kidding, right?"

"Do I look like I'm kidding?"

"Where are you going to find a better deal? I was willing to go out of my way to help you."

"I don't want your help. I want you to leave my office."

"You're just angry right now. We'll talk later, when you've had a chance to cool off."

"Good-bye, Thad." He left without another word.

Mona stepped inside. "Holy hell, I don't think I've ever seen Thad so pissed off. I'd like to thank you personally for that pleasure."

"Then you'll be tickled pink to know we won't be moving into his office after all."

"That's a relief," Mona said. "I won't have to share space with Bunnykins." She sat on the sofa. "So, why is Thad so angry?"

Finally, I told Mona everything. Her mouth kept forming little O's of surprise. "I've heard of Elizabeth Tyler Larkin," she said once I'd finished. "She's supposed to be this great philanthropist."

"She's also a very nice person."

"So where are we moving?"

"I'm trying to formulate a new plan."

"How about this plan," she said. "Once the truck is loaded tomorrow, ask your mom if you can store your things at the back of their workroom and we'll spend Saturday looking for a new office."

"I've been looking at offices for two months, Mona."

"I can help you."

I shook my head.

"You know what, Kate?" she said. "It's cool that you have all this pride, but you're not thinking of your patients. This isn't just about you."

I knew she was right. "I probably will spend Saturday looking for a place," I said, "but the location may not be the greatest. If I *do* find something affordable and in a decent location, it will probably be a one-room office. Just a place for me to see patients and nothing more," I added. "I may not have a reception area."

"Meaning I'll be out of a job," she said. "What if I *like* working here? Have you ever thought of that? Have you ever *once* considered that the people who care most about you might actually find joy in doing things for you? You make things more complicated than they have to be."

"I hope you're not mad at me," I said, "because almost everybody I know is mad at me right now."

In response, Mona reached across my desk, pulled a pen from my oversized coffee mug, and tossed it aside. It landed on the floor and rolled several inches as I stared, dumbfounded.

"There now," she said, planting her hands on her hips. "That leaves you with seven pens instead of eight."

I fought the urge to dive for the pen. "Well, *that* was a real mature thing to do."

I glared at her.

She glared back.

I don't know who cracked the first smile, but suddenly we were laughing. Mona sank onto the sofa and rolled back and forth as she howled with laughter. I swiped tears from my cheeks. Every time we tried to pull ourselves together, we fell into hearty guffaws.

"Stop!" I cried, holding my aching sides.

"Okay." She cleared her throat. "I'm okay now."

I turned in my chair so I wouldn't see the expression on her face.

The phone rang. I reached over to press the blinking button and accidentally hit the speaker one instead. I tried to correct my mistake, but the button was stuck. It should have come as no surprise since I often dropped food crumbs or spilled coffee on my phone and my computer keyboard. I continued to work on it as I picked up the phone.

"Kate, I'm so glad you're there," Uncle Bump said. "I have a serious problem on my hands. It's a delicate matter."

I looked at Mona and shrugged. She got up from the sofa and tried to get the button unstuck.

"What is it, Uncle Bump?" I asked.

He sighed. "Well, I've been having a little trouble in the bedroom. I can't seem to get, um, an erection."

Mona covered her mouth with both hands, even as her body shook with silent laughter.

"Oh, well," I said, swallowing hard to keep from joining Mona even though the absolute last thing in the world I wanted to think about was my uncle's inability to get a hard-on.

"To be perfectly honest, I've been having this problem for quite a while now," he confessed.

I turned my chair so that I was looking out the window instead of at Mona. Even though I hated it when my family called for medical advice that I could not give them, I found myself considering his dilemma. I couldn't imagine *any* man getting turned on by my aunt Lou, a woman who smoked unfiltered cigarettes, sounded like her vocal cords had gone through a shredder, and carried an ice pick in her purse. "I'm sorry to hear it," I said.

"So what I did was borrow some Viagra from a friend."

I heard a choking sound behind me. Mona had a sofa cushion pressed against her face. She raced out of the room and closed it behind her. I could hear her laughing from the other side.

"What's that noise?" Uncle Bump asked.

"Huh? Oh, they're having a big party in the next office." I got up and reached for the pen on the floor and stuffed it into the mug on my desk. I quickly counted to make certain I had an even number.

"Okay, so back to my problem," he said. "I was wondering if you thought it would be safe for me to take my friend's medicine."

"Gee, Uncle Bump, I don't know—"

"I'm thinking it would be safer than having your aunt mad at me," he said.

It was hard to believe that this was the same uncle who'd drunk and gotten into fistfights in the seediest bars in Atlanta. He'd earned the nickname "Bump" after a biker had broken his nose and left a tiny knot on the ridge. "Like I've said before, Uncle Bump, I'm not an MD. You need to talk to your doctor."

"I can't get an appointment for two weeks," he said. "If your aunt doesn't have an orgasm pretty soon she's liable to stick that ice pick through my liver."

"I'm sorry I can't help you," I said, "but I feel I should warn you that taking someone else's medication is never wise."

"I guess I'll have to take my chances," he said and hung up.

I reached into my drawer and pulled out my can of dust remover that was used to blast debris from keyboards, cell phone buttons, and a variety of electronic equipment. I sprayed it directly on the stuck button, and it finally popped up, cutting off the speakerphone.

I called my mother. She answered on the first ring. "Thanks for all your hard work," I said. "I'm sorry I wasn't here to help."

"Trixie and I were happy to do it."

"How's Arnie?"

"He insists on us calling him Arnell, and he is doing great. All he needed was a little TLC. So what time do you want to start loading the truck tomorrow?"

"I suppose we should start early," I said. I wasn't ready to break the news that I had no place to go. Maybe she'd feel sorry for me and let me operate my practice out of the back of her truck until I found something I could afford. Of course, it might prove difficult on rainy days.

We finished our conversation and hung up. I was

tired, and my stress level was at an all-time high. I wanted to talk to Jay in the worst way; but I would not push myself on him. And truly, I felt he owed me one or two explanations, starting with Mandy and ending with the reason he'd kept information from me about the fires.

I put my head on my desk. Maybe if I stayed perfectly still nothing dangerous or chaotic would happen.

I saw three patients back-to-back, which helped take my mind off my own problems, but by the end of the day I was dragging.

Mona tapped on the door and peeked in. "Guess who's here?"

"Tell me it's not a Jehovah's Witness," I said.

"Nope." She pushed open the door and Jeff stepped inside my office holding Mike.

He wore a big smile. "Your little princess was missing you so I thought I'd drop her off to save you a trip to my office. I hope you don't mind."

"Your timing is perfect," I said. Just seeing that Mike was okay lifted my spirits. Jeff put her down and she ran to me.

I scooped her up in my arms. "She's back to normal?" I asked, checking her eyes to see if they were glazed. She seemed alert and happy to see me.

"She's fine," Jeff said, grinning. I noticed Mona studying him from the doorway.

"Have you two met?" I asked.

I officially introduced them, and they shook hands.

"I sort of figured out who he was when he stepped inside holding Mike," Mona said. She looked at Jeff. "Just so you know, Kate is constantly singing your praises."

"The feeling is mutual," he said.

Mona suddenly gave a huge smile. "You know what I think?" she said. "We need to celebrate Mike's full recovery." She turned back to Jeff. "I don't know about you," she said to Jeff, "but Kate and I could use a little fun."

He seemed to consider it. "I could bring pizza," he suggested.

"And I'll bring wine," Mona said.

I was in no mood to celebrate. I was tired and irritable and figured I'd be terrible company. But they looked so hopeful that I hated to say no. I forced a smile. "You talked me into it," I said.

I was not surprised when Mona told me Dr. Hudson was on the phone. I knew I hadn't heard the last from him.

"I'm impressed, Dr. Holly," he said when I picked up, "that you were able to sneak a patient off the psychiatric ward. It proves how incompetent the hospital is."

"Yes, and that's one of our better hospitals," I said. "Scary, huh?" I added. "By the way, how's the nose?"

"You're going to pay for this," he said.

"Is that a threat, Dr. Hudson? Because if it is, I'm

going to hang up and call the police. Then, I'm going to call a friend of mine who is an investigative reporter, and once I steer him onto you and the senator, he'll blow this whole thing wide open. Let's see who loses whose license first."

"You can't prove anything."

"I have blood tests, photos of the bruises on Mrs. Larkin's body, and her side of the story. And while the senator may have paid off the housekeeper, she could be subpoenaed to testify in court."

"You're a real bitch on wheels, aren't you?"

"Well, I *do* have a bit of a temper," I said. "Hell, I blew up my own office two months ago with nitroglycerin. Which is why I'm being evicted from the building," I added, "and why you don't want to piss me off." I was amazed that I could sound like such a bad ass, especially with my knees knocking beneath my desk. "Go home, Dr. Hudson." I hung up.

chapter 12

....

Mona arrived at my place early, bearing two bottles of wine. I had taken a quick shower and changed into jeans and a knit pullover. Elizabeth Larkin had called to let me know she was okay and that she had an appointment with my psychiatrist friend first thing in the morning.

"I decided to bring a bottle of merlot since I don't know what Jeff drinks," Mona said. "Boy, is he good-looking or what? Have you ever noticed that all the really good looking guys are gay?"

"Not all of them."

"Okay, just most of them," she said.

I opened a bottle of chardonnay, poured two glasses, and led Mona to the sofa. She looked thoughtful.

"What's on your mind?" I asked. "I can see the wheels spinning in your brain."

"I was thinking about what you said about how I have a lot to offer, and that really made me feel good. Only problem is, I don't know what I should be doing with my life."

"What interests you most?" I asked.

"Other than online shopping?" she replied.

I took a sip of wine and waited.

"Let's face it, Kate. I'm shallow. I think that's why Liam has lost interest."

"He hasn't lost interest."

"He had dinner with a cute nurse last night. My PI got a picture of them."

I couldn't hide my disappointment. "Where did they go?"

Her bottom lip trembled. "The hospital cafeteria."

"Oh for Pete's sake!" I said. "That has to be the most unromantic place in the world."

"I know you think I'm overreacting, but my female intuition tells me something is going on between them. A woman's intuition is usually right. And why shouldn't he lose interest in me? He's devoted to helping people, and all I've done is complain about being ignored. Maybe he *was* ignoring me because he realized I have no, um, substance."

"I thought I was hard on myself," I said, "but I think you've got me beat."

She didn't seem to be listening. "I wasn't always this self-centered," she said. "I used to attend fundraisers all the time with Mr. Moneybags."

"So, go out and raise funds," I said. "I'll bet you know all the right people."

She looked at me. "You don't get it, Kate. The only reason I was accepted into that clique was because I was Mrs. Henry Epps. I'm not educated and refined. I'm the one who got kicked out of Miss Millie's Charm School, remember? And I would never have graduated from beauty school had I not promised my instructor a good time if he passed me." She looked as if she might cry. "I'm ashamed to say I was relieved he had a car wreck after graduation and ended up paralyzed from the waist down."

"You're making that up."

"It's the truth. The bottom line is you're the only real friend I have. You accept me just like I am."

"I don't believe that," I said. "People love being around you."

"Okay, the pool guy wants to be my friend, but I think he has ulterior motives."

"You might be onto something."

"I certainly don't fit in with Liam's friends," she continued. "I thought a femur was an exotic cat, and a corpuscle was a military person. His friends think I'm an idiot. I figured if I went to nursing school I would be able to talk on their level, you know?" She shook her head. "But I wouldn't last five minutes in nursing school, and the reason I've got a PI following Liam is so I can catch him doing something wrong and break up with him before he breaks up with me."

I saw that she was fighting tears. "You know what, Mona? I don't care how smart Liam's friends are or how cute the nurses may be, they've got nothing on you. If you were all invited to a party, *you* would be the one to stand out. Why? Because you're witty and beautiful and because you have a heart of gold."

"But I would never take in a stray dog or risk losing my license by sneaking a patient from the psychiatric ward," she said. "You could have had a luxury office at Thad's place and built a fine practice, but you refused to go along with him and do the easy thing. You did the *right* thing," she added.

"I know you, Mona," I said. "You would have done the same thing. You would have gone to any extreme to help an emotionally and physically battered woman find safety."

I noticed we'd finished our wine and I went into the kitchen to refill our glasses. The phone rang. Jeff spoke from the other end of the line.

"I had to go back to the office for a small emergency," he said. "I'm running about twenty minutes late."

"That's fine," I said. "If you're lucky we'll still have a little wine left."

I carried our glasses to the living room and set them down on the coffee table. I turned on the radio and chose a soft rock station, hoping it would lift Mona's spirits as well as mine.

By the time Jeff arrived with pizza and ice cream, Mona and I had opened the merlot and we were each on our third glass of wine. I'd turned up the music. I was feeling tipsy. It occurred to me that I'd eaten nothing all day.

"How about a drink," Mona said to Jeff as the three of us stood in the kitchen. She motioned to the bottle of wine.

"Sure," he said. "Here, let me pour it." He reached for the bottle, and his hand brushed Mona's. He looked embarrassed.

The radio started playing "Old Time Rock and Roll," and Mona ran to the living room. "This is my favorite song!" She turned it up loud. "Kate, come dance with me."

I looked at Jeff. "We're a little drunk, I think."

He grinned. "So, go dance."

I kicked off my shoes and joined Mona in the living room. Jeff watched from the doorway; Mike stood beside him wagging her tail. She came into the living room and barked several times as if wanting to join in.

"Ignore her," I told Mona. "She's probably still got a buzz going."

The song stopped, and another one came on, "Slow Dancing." Mona motioned for Jeff. "Come dance with me, handsome," she said, holding her arms out.

I don't know if he looked more surprised or confused, but he set his wineglass down and hurried toward her. I picked up Mike and pretended to dance with her as her tail wagged happily. I closed my eyes and thought of the slow dances I'd shared with Jay, and I was suddenly filled with a sense of longing so deep it took my breath away. I wanted to call him in the worst way. I gripped Mike tighter.

The song stopped. "You're an excellent dancer, Jeff," I heard Mona say.

"I had a good partner. Do you want me to refill your glass?"

"That would be nice."

I reached into the cabinet for plates and set the table as they joined me in the kitchen, chatting about their favorite songs. I noticed Mona's words had lost their edge and they sounded soft around the corners.

"Dinner is served," I announced as I set the pizza box on the table. I noticed Jeff had finished his glass of red wine. "Does anyone want a soft drink?"

"I'll take one," he said.

Mona shook her head. "I'm good."

I grabbed two soft drinks from the refrigerator. Jeff pulled out our chairs, and we sat down. I opened the box and placed a slice of pizza on everyone's plate.

"This is really nice," Mona said. "I haven't been out in a long time."

"How come?" Jeff asked.

"I've been in a relationship. A dead-end relationship," she added, taking a long sip of her wine.

"You don't know that," I said, wishing Mona would put down her wine and start eating her pizza.

"Don't ever date anyone younger than you," Mona told Jeff. "It's very stressful."

"Mona, would you like Parmesan cheese on your pizza?" I asked, offering her the shaker.

"I'm good," she repeated. She looked at Jeff. "How old do I look to you?"

I gave an inward sigh.

"Twenty-nine?" he asked.

"I'm thirty-two. Same as Kate," she added.

"You both look very young."

That was the thing about Jeff, I thought. He always knew the right thing to say.

Mona emptied her wineglass. "Do you have any idea how much Botox has been injected into this face?" she asked him, slurring her words badly. She held up her glass for Jeff to refill it. He looked at me.

"Your pizza is getting cold," I told her.

"I'm not hungry," she said.

Jeff took her glass, got up from the table, and poured the wine. I noticed when he handed it to her that it was only half full. I smiled at him.

Mona leaned across the table. "So, Jeff, tell me about yourself," she said. "Are you involved with anyone?"

I immediately tensed.

"Actually, I'm too busy to think about having a relationship," he said. He looked at me. "I put an ad in the newspaper hoping to find someone interested in sharing my practice."

"Good for you!" I said.

"It must be hard for someone like you to meet someone," Mona said.

"I think you've had enough wine," I told her, taking her glass.

"You're right," she said and came to her feet. "I

should go." She looked at Jeff. "Just so you know, I don't normally act like such a lush." She wobbled. Jeff and I jumped up and steadied her so she wouldn't fall.

"No way are you getting behind the steering wheel of a car," I said, irritated that she had probably embarrassed Jeff and put a sour note on what was supposed to have been a fun evening. Normally, I chose to have my pity parties alone so I wouldn't drag others down with me.

"I'll drive her home," Jeff said.

I couldn't hide my annoyance as I handed Mona her purse. "Do you need to use the bathroom or anything before you go?"

She shook her head. "I probably won't throw up until I get home."

"Please take the pizza with you," I told Jeff. "There's plenty left."

"No, just keep it. I might have to go back to the office later."

He and I helped Mona to his car. Once I saw that her seat belt was fastened securely, I closed the door. "I'm really sorry," I told him, and prayed Mona would not say anything to embarrass him on the ride home.

"Don't worry about it, Kate." He took my hand and squeezed it, then hurried around to his side of the car and got in.

Inside, I wrapped the pizza and put it in the refrigerator. The wine I'd drunk had given me a pounding headache, and the day had suddenly caught up with me, leaving me exhausted. I took two aspirin and lay down on the sofa. Mike jumped up and curled against my feet. I closed my eyes and tried to make everything go away.

I don't know how long I'd been asleep when the kitchen phone rang and yanked me from a sweet dream I'd been having of Jay. I realized I'd fallen asleep on the sofa. I bolted up and hurried into the kitchen, cursing when I stubbed my toe on a chair leg.

I could feel it throbbing as I answered.

"Kate, you'll never believe what has happened," my mother said from the other end. I could tell she'd been crying. I instantly became awake.

"What it is?" I asked.

"It's Trixie," she said, bursting into tears. "She has eloped with Slick Eddie."

I flipped on the kitchen light and squinted at the clock over the stove. Five a.m. "When?" I asked.

"She didn't come home last night. I didn't get much sleep because I kept listening for her to come home. I just now got up and decided to make coffee. There was a note from her in the canister, telling me that she and Eddie were flying to Vegas to get married!"

I sat down in a chair at the kitchen table. My head felt fuzzy. "I'm sorry, Mom," I said, not knowing what else to say, at the same time wishing I could get my

hands on Eddie Franks. He had taken advantage of my
naive aunt. "Give me time to grab a quick shower, and
I'll be over," I said and hung up. I ran upstairs.

I was thankful that traffic was light. I reached my
mom and aunt's studio in Little Five Points in record
time. I pulled behind the building and climbed the
back stairs to their apartment. Arnie met me at the back
door, wearing what looked to be one of my mother's
old house dresses and a pair of fuzzy bedroom slip-
pers. He hugged me and stepped back so I could enter.
"Would you like coffee?" he asked.

"I'd kill for it."

My mother was sitting at the kitchen table staring
into space. I hugged her from behind. She took my hand
and held it. "I never thought Trixie would do something
like this," she said. "Marry a man she has known less
than a week."

I took a chair at the antique claw-foot kitchen table
that I knew had come from an estate sale. Almost everything my mother and aunt owned had come from
estate sales, garage sales, and flea markets, which is
why both their place and mine were a mishmash of
furnishings.

I was shocked by the lines of grief on my mother's
face. She looked old. "I'm sorry," I said as Arnie set a
mug of coffee in front of me. I noted he'd gotten a
French manicure since I'd last seen him.

"It's my fault," my mother said. "I complained all

the time about Slick Eddie. I ended up pushing your aunt right into his arms."

"It's not the end of the world, Mom," I said. "Maybe it was love at first sight."

"There's no such thing," she grumbled. "That only happens on *The Young and the Restless*."

I thought of Jay, the way it had felt the night he'd kissed me for the first time. That kiss had changed me forever. "Not necessarily," I said.

Arnie joined us at the table. "I could be wrong," he said, "but what I think your mother is feeling right now is a sense of betrayal. Isn't that right, Dixie?"

She reached for his hand and squeezed it. "You're so sensitive, Arnell," she said. She mopped her eyes. "That's the thing about being someone's twin. You feel like you know that person as well as you know yourself."

She blew her nose and continued. "Trixie and I never kept secrets. We could almost read each other's minds." She looked at me. "Trixie knew I was in love with your father before I knew it. She even knew I was pregnant with you before I told her. That's how it was with us, until lately," she added.

I put my hand on hers. "Mom, I know you're hurt, but there are worse things than having a family member, even your twin, elope," I said. "We're going to have to accept it."

"You know what I think we should do?" Arnie said.

She looked at him. "Hire a hit man to go after Slick Eddie?"

"I think we should throw a wedding reception for Trixie and Eddie," he said.

My mom's mouth formed a large O, but nothing came out. Arnie put his finger beneath her chin and forced her mouth closed.

"He's right, Mom," I said. "We have to support Aunt Trixie. I've seen too many families disrupted or destroyed because one person didn't accept another."

Arnie nodded. "Yeah, look what happened to me."

"You can't afford to alienate your own twin," I told her. "Think what that would do to both of you." My mother looked at me as though I were speaking a foreign language. "We could have a small party," I said. "Nothing fancy."

"I could prepare heavy hors d'oeuvres," Arnie said, "so we wouldn't have to worry about a sit-down dinner. I know just the person I can ask to bake a wedding cake. Not one of those froufrou-looking cakes; just something simple. Also, I have a friend who can get champagne at cost. I would take care of it all," he added, "as a wedding gift for Trixie and Eddie."

We all waited for my mother to say something. Finally, she sighed. "That's very nice of you, Arnell," she said. "I suppose I have no choice but to try and be happy for Trixie because I'm not going to risk losing her. Even if I have to *pretend* to like her lousy husband," she added. "Even if I have to bite my tongue clean off to keep from telling him how I really feel."

"Eddie might surprise you, Mom," I said. "What if he turns out to be a great brother-in-law?" Of course,

Eddie and I were going to have a long talk when I got him alone, I reminded myself. I was already lining up in my mind all that I would threaten him with if he hurt my aunt: his life, prison, or castration by my aunt Lou.

We began planning the party. "I would suggest something small and intimate if you want to have the party here," Arnie said. "Say, no more than twenty-five guests. Otherwise, you're going to have to rent a place."

"I like the sound of small and intimate," my mother said. I could tell she was beginning to relax. "How are we going to know when to hold the party?" she asked. "Trixie didn't tell me in her note if she and Eddie were planning a honeymoon."

"Aunt Trixie will call you," I assured her.

Arnie nodded in agreement. "But I can get a lot done in the meantime," he said. "I can make food up ahead of time and freeze it."

My mother got up and reached into a drawer for a spiral notebook. She began making a guest list of those she would invite to the party. She looked at me. "I suppose I'll have to invite your uncle Bump and his nutso wife," she said, "but I'm not inviting Lucien. The guests would lose their appetites if they had to look at all his pierced body parts," she added.

We mulled over the list for an hour when the front door suddenly opened and Aunt Trixie walked in with Eddie behind her.

My mother bolted to her feet, a shocked expression on her face. "Be nice, Mom," I said under my breath.

191

She hurried across the room and threw her arms around Trixie's neck. "Congratulations!" she said. She hesitated only briefly before hugging Eddie. Arnie and I did the same.

"I hope the two of you will have a wonderfully happy life together," he said.

Trixie's face flamed red. "Um, thank you," she said, "but we're not married."

My mother gaped. "What!"

"We didn't go through with it."

chapter 13

....

My mother was speechless at first. "What do you mean, you didn't go through with it? We've already planned your party. We've decided on the guest list."

"We changed our minds," Trixie said.

My mother planted her hands on her ample hips. "Trixie, this is just like you," she said. "You leave a note telling me you've eloped, and just when I've planned a beautiful party for you, I find out you changed your mind. How could you do this to me?" she demanded. "You've ruined everything!"

I looked at my mom and realized there was no way to win.

Eddie stepped forward. "It's my fault, Dixie," he said. "I'm in love with your sister, which is why I decided we shouldn't get married right now."

My mother looked from me to Arnie. "Does that

make sense to either of you? Because it doesn't make a darn bit of sense to me."

Eddie gazed down at the floor. "I did some things in the past that I'm not proud of," he said. "I don't want to marry your sister until I make them right."

The room was silent. I stared at Eddie in disbelief. Inside, I was jumping for joy. I had been waiting for a long time to hear those words come out of his mouth. Remorse.

I arrived at the office and found Mona wearing sunglasses. "Are you okay?" I asked.

She shook her head. "I am so hung over I get dizzy every time I stand up."

"I'm sorry to hear it," I said, although I had trouble mustering up any sympathy at all.

"I did something terrible last night," she whispered.

"I was there, remember?"

"No, it gets worse." Her cheeks turned red. "I kissed Jeff. More than once," she added.

I didn't know what to say at first. "Well, that's not so terrible," I said. "I think," I added.

"Don't you get it? I tried to make out with a gay guy!"

"I get it, Mona."

"I think I embarrassed him. I'll never be able to face him again." She suddenly covered her mouth. Her eyes widened in horror.

"What?"

She moved her hand. "Does that make me a lesbian?"

I gave a massive sigh. "No, Mona, you're not a lesbian. You're just a very confused person."

I'd barely gotten the words out before the door opened and in walked Jeff. He had Mona's wallet in his hand. He looked at her. "You left this in my car last night."

"Oh no!" Mona said and ducked beneath her desk.

Jeff looked at me.

"She's embarrassed," I said. "She told me what happened."

He shook his head, walked around the desk, and looked down at Mona. "Please don't be embarrassed," he said. "You had a little too much to drink, that's all."

"You're damn right I did!" she said. "You should have stopped me from making a big fat fool of myself."

Jeff ducked beneath the desk and tried to reason with her. The phone rang, and I answered it. My aunt Lou spoke from the other end. Her voice sounded as though it had been through a wood chipper.

"Your uncle has a slight problem," she said. "He took Viagra last night, and while I am pleased to say that it worked very well, he still has an erection. I wanted to ask you if you think that is normal."

I buried the sigh that threatened to escape my lips. What the hell did *I* know about normal? "Aunt Lou, we've gone over this before. I'm not a medical doctor."

"Well, you're no help," she snapped.

I had counted on this being a good day. "I think you should take Uncle Bump to the ER and have someone look at him."

"That's exactly what I told him," she said, "but he's too embarrassed. His thingy is sticking straight out. He can't even zip his pants."

The last thing I wanted to think of was my uncle's thingy. "Perhaps he could wear an overcoat," I suggested.

"Hmm," she said. "I didn't think of that. I guess it goes without saying that Bump is not going to be able to help you move today unless the swelling goes down. And I wouldn't count on Lucien and his band either. They have bad hangovers."

"There seems to be a lot of that going around," I said before she hung up.

I could hear Mona crying from beneath her desk, and the more Jeff tried to reason with her, the louder she got. I had to assume part of it was due to her fear of losing Liam.

The door to the reception room opened and my mother, aunt, and Arnie walked through. They looked as tired as I felt after what we'd gone through over the now-canceled nuptials.

All three paused when they heard Mona sobbing from her hiding place. "You should have stopped me from kissing you!" Mona shouted at Jeff.

"I tried," he said, "but you were like an octopus!"

"Excuse me!" she said.

"Mona? Jeff?" I said. "You might want to settle this later."

"I don't want what happened last night to interfere with our friendship," Jeff said.

"We don't *have* a friendship!" she said.

"Jeff?" I called out louder. "We have company."

They peered out from under the desk simultaneously. "Oh no!" Mona cried. "Now everybody knows I acted like a drunken whore last night." She disappeared once more.

My mom looked at me. "This is what I'm talking about," she said. "Every time I walk through this door there is something crazy going on. You should have joined us in the junk business when you had a chance." She stepped closer to the desk. "Mona, get the H-E-L-L out from under that desk."

Mona did as she was told. "I am so embarrassed," she said.

"Don't beat yourself up," Aunt Trixie said. "Last night, I almost married an ex-con who jilted several women out of their retirement funds. Nobody is perfect."

"She's right," Arnie said. "It could be worse. At least you're not a man trapped in a woman's body."

Jeff checked his wristwatch. "I have to go," he said. He looked at Mona. "You're a lot of fun to be around," he said. "I'd like to put this behind us if we could." He smiled at me and hurried out.

My mother looked around. "Where are Bump and Lucien?"

"Uncle Bump can't make it," I said, swallowing a smile. "Something came up. And we can forget about Lucien as well."

The door opened, and I was stunned when Jay walked through. "What are *you* doing here?" I asked.

"I'm here to help you move."

"You are?"

He shrugged. "I figured it was the right thing to do."

"We need to talk," I said, pulling him inside my office. I closed the door. "Why didn't you tell me the arsonist was targeting firefighters?"

He arched one brow. "You have to ask?"

I decided we could save that discussion for later. "I think I know who is setting the fires," I said. "Ronnie Sumner."

Jay frowned. "What? Why would you think that?"

"He lied about his divorce. His wife died in a house fire. Their house," I added.

"The water heater blew up in her face."

"You already know?" I asked, surprised.

"He asked me to keep it confidential. The reason he left Houston was because he got tired of dealing with the looks of pity. It has been hard enough for him to rebuild his life without the constant reminder."

"Oh."

Jay frowned. "Who told you?" he asked.

"Carter Atkins."

"Dammit, Kate! I told you to stay away from him. Can't you do one simple thing I ask?"

"But Jay—"

"I'm this close to having Carter arrested for trying to plant evidence in Sumner's locker."

"Carter claims he was *looking* for evidence."

"Oh, so you and Carter are investigating the arsons now," he said. "That will be good news to the team of experts assigned to the case."

"Don't you find it odd that the fires didn't start until Ronnie moved back?"

"What I find odd is that you're getting in the middle of something that doesn't concern you."

"How can you say it doesn't concern me?" I said in disbelief. "Unless I've already been replaced by Mandy," I added.

He suddenly looked frustrated. "You know what? I don't have time for this." He reached for the doorknob. "We've got to load your things on the truck and move you to lover boy's office."

"I'm not moving in with Thad," I said.

It was Jay's turn to look surprised. "That's the first sane thing that has come out of your mouth. Where *are* you moving?"

"I don't know. I'm going to ask my mom if I can put my things in their storage room until I find something. Once I update her on the situation," I added, remembering I hadn't yet mentioned the change of plans.

We left my office. "Where did everybody go?" I asked Mona, who had seemingly pulled herself together.

"They're loading the truck. Oh, and Elizabeth Larkin just called to let you know she really liked the psychiatrist you set her up with. She said she was feeling a lot better and planned to ask you and Thad to dinner next week."

"That's nice." I didn't have time to think about next week, I reminded myself.

"I told her you were moving, only you had no idea where because Thad had turned out to be such a jerk. She felt awful for you. Thad's name has been taken off her invitation list."

"I'm glad you didn't burden her with my problems," I said.

Mona went on. "I also asked if she and I could get together sometime soon so I could pick her brain since she has helped so many underprivileged children with her fund-raisers." Mona looked at Jay. "I'm trying to find my reason for existing."

"I thought you were going to be a nurse."

"I'm pretty sure nurses aren't allowed to wear nail polish," she said.

Jay nodded as though it made perfect sense. He stacked several boxes on top of each other and started for the door. I hurried to open it, but my mother beat me to it. She stepped back and held it open for him. Trixie and Arnie followed her inside.

"Mom, I have something to tell you," I said. "I don't really have a place to move to yet." I explained the situation. "I was hoping I could store my stuff in the back of the workroom."

"Why does everything have to be so complicated with you, Kate?" she said.

"Of course you can store your things at our place," Trixie said. "We have plenty of space. Dixie and I can help you look for an office over the weekend."

Jay returned with a dolly and slipped it beneath a file cabinet. He rolled it out. Arnie carried another load downstairs, and I grabbed a box. We took the freight elevator down. With everybody working, it took less than an hour to pack the truck. "I'll follow you in my car," I said.

Mona grabbed her purse. "I'll ride with you."

"I'll be right behind you," Jay said.

We followed my mother's truck, caravan-style, to Little Five Points, made room at the back of the work-room, and unloaded.

"We have a bunch of fried chicken left over from last night," my mom said, "not to mention Arnell's special potato salad. How about we all go up for lunch?"

It sounded like a good plan since I was hungry. I'd only eaten half a slice of my pizza the night before, having lost my appetite after Mona's display.

Inside the kitchen, my mother and aunt began pulling food from the refrigerator, including baked beans and deviled eggs. They placed everything on the kitchen counter to create a buffet.

Jay chuckled. "That's quite a spread you've got there."

"Well, I was just in one of my cooking moods," my mother said. "I like to show off in front of Arnell," she added with a smile. "Everybody dig in. Don't be shy. A couple of you will have to eat in the living room since we don't have enough chairs at the kitchen table."

The women ended up sitting in the kitchen, and Jay and Arnie sat in the living room. I wondered what Jay made of Arnie's Capri slacks and blouse, but if he thought it strange, he didn't mention it. Jay was obviously accustomed to strange when it came to people he met through me.

"Thank you for the great lunch," he said once he finished eating. He dumped his chicken bones in the trash and put his plate in the sink. "I need to go home and grab a quick nap."

"You look tired," my mother said as he hugged her and my aunt. "Please be careful."

I walked him to the door. "Thank you for all your help."

"I was glad to do it." He hurried down the stairs without another word.

"Things are pretty tense between you and Jay," my mom said. "I was hoping you'd have worked it all out by now."

My aunt looked at her. "It's none of our business, Dixie. Kate is perfectly capable of solving her own problems, and she doesn't need us to butt in."

My mother looked astonished but said nothing.

I tried to hide my smile. I was proud of my aunt for standing up to her. I began loading the dishwasher, but Trixie stopped me. "I can do that," she said.

I nodded my thanks. "I have to run back to the office and clean up."

"I plan to help you," Mona said.

I knew she was trying to suck up after the previous night, so I didn't argue. She got into my car. We said very little on the way. We were both shocked to find the streets blocked with crime scene tape two blocks from my office building. "What in the world is going on?" I said, noting that police cars and fire trucks were parked a short distance away. News cameras were perched on top of vans. It looked like a scene out of a movie.

"It must be bad," Mona said.

It took forever to find a parking space. Mona and I hurried toward a crowd of onlookers. I recognized a young dental assistant who worked in an office down the hall from me. "What happened?" I asked her.

"Someone discovered a bomb right in front of our building!" she said. "The police have evacuated the surrounding area."

"A bomb!" Mona and I said in unison.

"Was anyone hurt?" I asked.

She shook her head. "I heard this guy saw it when he got out of his car. He almost stepped on it. Can you imagine what would have happened if he had?"

"How long ago?" Mona asked.

"An hour, maybe longer," the young woman said. "The guy who saw it thought it looked suspicious and called the police from his cell phone. The police called the bomb squad, and they sent in a robot. Can you believe it?" she added.

Mona's cell phone rang. She pulled it from her purse and answered. I saw her eyes widen as she listened. She gulped. "Are you sure?"

"What's wrong?" I asked.

She shot me a look of pure horror.

"Mona?"

She suddenly looked angry. "Let me tell you something, you pathetic excuse for a PI," she sputtered into the phone. "You'd better keep my name out of it or I'll sue your pants off, you got that? I'll hang you out to dry. By the time I'm finished with you, you'll wish you never met me." She hung up and fixed me with determined look. "I have to leave the country!" she said. "Would you drive me to the airport?"

"Why don't you tell me what's going on first?"

She pulled me away from the crowd. "It's the worst thing that could possibly happen," she said. "The PI tracked Liam to our building, then lost him. The live GPS fell off Liam's car. The PI said it was hard finding a place to attach the GPS since Liam has that little economy car."

"Mona, you're not making sense!"

"Liam thought the GPS was a bomb and called the police, who called the bomb squad. You need to take me to the bank so I can withdraw some money before we go to the airport. I'll have to get a new identity. What do you think of the name Juanita?"

"Hold it!" I said. "How could police mistake a GPS for a bomb?"

"The PI said it was in a small camouflaged case with a cell phone inside."

"How did he find out it had been reported as a bomb?"

"He has a police scanner in his car. He heard the location and already knew where Liam and the GPS were. He's got more stuff than the FBI, Kate. Anyway, he is on his way to the police station to clear it up. He promised not to mention my name, but I know what goes on in interrogations. I watch *The Closer* with Kyra Sedgwick. He'll sing like a canary."

She suddenly burst into tears.

"What *now*?" I said.

"I feel terrible about this. Not only did it probably scare the hell out of Liam, but think how terrified all these poor people must've been when they had to evacuate." She looked at the crowd. "This is all my fault. I am a bad person!"

I grabbed her by the shoulders and shook her. "Stop it!" I said. "You're not thinking straight. This is *not* your fault, and you are *not* a bad person. This is your PI's fault for doing a crappy job."

"But I hired him to do it."

"People do it all the time, Mona. How do you think spouses catch their mates cheating on them? Besides, your PI is legally bound by client confidentiality laws. He *can't* mention your name." At least I was fairly certain that was the case.

Suddenly, a loudspeaker squawked. "Let's move

closer," I said, tugging Mona toward the crowd so we could hear.

"May I have your attention please," a male voice said. "The bomb squad has determined that the suspicious case found in the parking lot is not a threat. It has been removed from the premises, and the buildings are safe to enter. Again, the object found in the parking lot has been removed. You are free to return to your offices."

The people looked about as the message was repeated several times. Two policemen began taking down the crime scene tape.

"See? Everything is going to be okay," I said.

We started walking toward the building as Mona brushed tears from her face. "I'm going to have to live with this guilt for the rest of my life."

"Then you're an idiot!" I said. I took her arm and pulled her to a stop. "Now listen closely, Mona. We are not going to tell anyone about this, do you understand?"

"Not even my priest?" she said.

"You're not Catholic, for Pete's sake!"

"But what if I decide to become a Catholic one day and I have to go to confession?"

I closed my eyes. I told myself that Mona was in shock, and that's why she wasn't thinking straight. "Mona?" I said, mustering the last of my patience.

"Okay, I'll become a Presbyterian instead."

"Mona!"

We both turned at the sound of Liam's voice. He

waved and headed our way. "Keep your mouth shut," I warned Mona.

"Okay, but you have to promise not to tell him I tried to make out with a gay guy," she said out of the side of her mouth.

Liam was carrying roses. "Sweetheart, I've been looking all over for you," he said. "These are for you."

"They are?" she said, taking them.

"To thank you for putting up with me these past few weeks while we were short-staffed at the hospital."

She laughed brightly. "Don't be silly, Liam. You're a medical student and an intern. I expect you to be busy."

Liam looked at me. "Hi, Kate. Am I a lucky man or what? Most women wouldn't understand my crazy schedule, but Mona—" He paused. "She's a real trouper."

"She certainly is," I said, giving her a jovial slap on the back.

He kissed her. "You two are *not* going to believe what happened to me." He filled us in quickly, then checked his wristwatch. "I have to go," he said after we'd heard the story for the second time. He kissed Mona again. "How about I take you to dinner tonight? Say around seven?"

She nodded dumbly and he hurried away.

"You so owe me," I told her. I started toward the building once more with Mona on my heels. I spotted my landlord, Mr. Green. "Oh great," I muttered. "Just the man I wanted to see. Tell me I'm having a nightmare."

Green saw Mona and me as we approached the double glass doors. He was completely bald except for the hair growing out of his ears.

"Well, Dr. Holly," he said. "I was on my way to see if you'd cleaned your ex-office before I put locks on the door."

"I got sidetracked," I said. "But feel free to lock it. I'm not in the mood to clean it, anyway."

"I guess you heard about the bomb scare," he said. "I figured one of your crazies had something to do with it."

I crossed my arms. "I resent that remark," I said.

He pointed at me. "And you're even crazier and more dangerous than the lunatics you treat."

Several of the tenants on the way back into the building stopped and stared. I knew most of them because they attended the open house each month.

A man I recognized from attending the monthly event stepped forward and got in Green's face. "I'm an attorney, and not only have you slandered Dr. Holly in front of all these people, you just made a discriminatory remark regarding the mentally ill. Bad mistake, pal, since my wife has been in therapy the past three years for clinical depression," he added.

"I didn't mean anything by it," Green said.

The attorney whipped out a small notepad and pen and looked at the crowd. "Would those of you who heard the comments made by this person please write down your names and addresses."

The president of the bank reached for the pad. He

was big on the chocolate éclairs we served. He glared at Green. "Do you know who I am?" he demanded before scribbling his name.

Green nodded.

"Well, I happen to be in treatment myself," he said, "and I'll have your sorry butt on a platter before it's over." He passed the pad to the next person.

Green looked at me. "I'm sorry," he said. "I misspoke. I could lose my job," he added, almost in a whisper.

"You expect me to defend you?" I said in disbelief. "You evicted me."

He looked pale. "I might reconsider if you'll tell these people I'm not as bad as they think I am."

"I would need that in writing," I said, even as the crowd continued to pass the notebook around.

"Give me two minutes." He ran to his car. He was out of breath when he returned bearing a thin sheath of papers. "This is a lease," he said. "I'll agree to anything."

"I want a three-year lease with no rent increase."

"You got it." He began writing quickly.

I suddenly felt brave. "And I want the office painted in taupe and new carpet installed this weekend so I can move in on Monday."

"What!" He frowned.

"Take it or leave it," I said.

"That's blackmail!"

"No it's not," the attorney said. "It's called negotiation."

"Okay!" Green replied. He added my demands.

"Don't sign it yet," the attorney said. He glanced around. "Is anyone a notary?"

A woman raised her hand. "I'll be right back." She hurried inside the building. The attorney read through the lease. "Everything looks to be in order."

The woman returned with her supplies and witnessed our signatures. "I'll need a couple more witnesses," she said. The bank president and the young dental assistant stepped forward. Once they'd signed the lease, Green reached for it.

"Not so fast," the attorney said. "Dr. Holly is going to need a copy."

"I'll make a copy," the notary offered and hurried inside the building once again. She returned and handed Green and me a copy.

"May I have the pages from the notebook?" Green asked the attorney.

He shook his head. "Nope. I plan to keep it on file in case you give Dr. Holly any more problems."

"That's blackmail," Green said for the second time.

"You might be right." The attorney tucked the pages inside his jacket and went into the building.

Green stormed away, cursing under his breath.

I looked at Mona. "I think that went rather well." The last word barely left my mouth before my knees went weak. Several people grabbed my arms and led me inside to the elevator.

chapter 14

······························

I slept until noon on Saturday. I suppose I'd been tense for so long that I was physically and emotionally done in. I plodded downstairs and made coffee. From the window I saw Mike sleeping in a patch of sunlight. I noted the light blinking on my answering machine, but I was determined to drink my first cup in silence. I sat on my sofa and propped my legs on the coffee table. I savored the moment. It felt like forever since I'd had time to enjoy even the smallest pleasures.

I poured my second cup and pressed the button on my machine.

"Kate, this is your mother." I did a mental eye roll. Like I wouldn't recognize her voice, I thought. "Arnell is making chicken parmesan and Caesar salad for Sunday dinner. You're welcome to join us tomorrow. Call me back."

The machine beeped and Mona spoke. "My PI called late last night. Everything worked out, and my name is not going to be dragged into you-know-what so I don't have to leave the country after all. And Liam and I had a wonderful evening last night." She paused. "I'm meeting Elizabeth Larkin for lunch, so if you need me you can call me on my cell phone."

I waited for my next message.

"Katie, I heard your landlord is going to let you stay in the office after all," Jay said. "Don't worry about moving your things back in tomorrow. I've got a couple of guys and a truck lined up. We can have you moved in no time."

I was touched by his message. Despite everything, Jay made it plain I was a high priority in his life.

I had a couple more calls, and a hang-up. I was too tired to call anyone back, but I knew if I didn't return my mother's call she would think I had been murdered in my sleep and would send the police to my house.

"You sound terrible!" she said. "Have you got the flu? I'll bet you forgot to take the flu shot. I'll bet you didn't write a reminder on your calendar."

"I'm not sick, Mom. Just tired. But I wanted to let you know that I'd love to come to dinner tomorrow."

"We'll set an extra plate at the table," she said. "Try to rest."

I hung up, made a sandwich, and started upstairs just as the phone rang again. I didn't feel like talking so I listened to the message.

"Bitsy Stout here. I just found another pile of poop

in my yard. You're asking for trouble, lady. You *and* your ugly dog," she added.

I yanked the phone from the receiver. "Don't call my dog ugly!" I yelled. I hung up and went back to bed.

I awoke the following morning at eight, still feeling tired. I'd slept on and off the day before, returning phone messages in between. I found Mike stretched out on the rug in front of the kitchen sink, gnawing a rawhide bone.

The phone rang. Jay spoke from the other end. He didn't waste time with preliminaries. "We should arrive at the office with your things around five p.m.," he said. "You'll need to be there with a key to let us in."

"You sound tired," I said.

"I'm okay. I have to run so I'll see you then."

The phone clicked, and I heard a dial tone. "I love you madly too, Jay," I muttered and hung up.

I showered and dressed in jeans and a blouse. While I was deliriously happy that I didn't have to move to another office after all, I dreaded unpacking my things. Just thinking about it made me even more tired. I decided to take a nap.

I arrived at my mom and aunt's, fresh-cut flowers in hand, just in time for Sunday dinner.

My mother made a big fuss. "You didn't have to buy these."

"I wanted to," I said. "I can't thank you guys enough for all you've done."

Arnie was dressed in jeans, a glittery tank top, and a lamé scarf. "Speaking for myself, it was my pleasure," he said. "Now, everybody sit down so I can serve the Caesar salads."

We took our place at the table. Aunt Trixie looked at me. "Eddie wanted to join us, but he is volunteering at the soup kitchen in town," she said.

"How nice," I said. I looked at my mother, who gave me a quick eye roll.

"Would you like fresh black pepper on your salad?" she asked, offering me the pepper mill.

Arnie smiled in delight as we praised his salad, chicken parmesan, and spinach pasta. "That was a fabulous meal," I said as I cleared the table. "I don't remember when I've eaten so much. Would you consider moving in with me?"

"He can't move in with you because he's moving in with us," Aunt Trixie said. "We've adopted him."

"For real?" I asked.

Arnie blushed. "It's tempting. I've become rather fond of your mother and aunt. I feel like I finally belong. Is everyone ready for dessert? I call it Chocolate Sin."

Despite swearing I could not hold another bite, I ate my entire dessert and part of my mom's. Once again, my eyelids felt heavy. I couldn't stop yawning.

"Kate, go lie down on my bed and take a nap," my mother said.

I shook my head in bewilderment. "All I've done for two days is sleep," I said. "Besides, I need to be awake when Jay arrives. He and a few guys from the department are coming by to move my things back to the office, and I have to meet them at five to let them in."

"He already called us," she said. "I'll wake you in plenty of time."

I didn't have to be told twice. I went into my mother's bedroom, where the scent of Chantilly, her favorite perfume, sweetened the air. I curled up like a fat cat on her plump feather mattress. I started to drift. I was vaguely aware when she came in and covered me with a light quilt.

I felt I'd been asleep for a long time when someone touched me gently on the shoulder. I found my mom standing over me. "It's four o'clock," she whispered. "I thought you'd like a cup of coffee before you leave." She brushed my hair from my face and stroked it with her fingers.

"Mom?"

She looked at me.

"Thanks again for everything."

She sat on the edge of the bed and continued to stroke my hair. "You're so much like me, Kate," she said, "whether you want to believe it or not. When your father first died, I felt like I had to be so strong. After all, I had to raise you. People tried to help, but I was too prideful. It never occurred to me that I was stealing their joy by refusing to allow them to do things for us."

I nodded as I recalled hearing those same words from Mona when I refused her help only days earlier.

After a quick cup of coffee, my mother and Aunt Trixie slipped on their sweaters and Arnie donned a shawl.

"We're going with you," my mother said. "You might need help unpacking all your books." I opened my mouth to protest, but she cut me off. "Remember what we just talked about?" she said.

Arnie rode in the truck with my mother, and Aunt Trixie joined me in my car. "So, do you plan to keep dating Eddie?" I asked once we were on our way.

"I'll see him as a friend," she said, "but I don't want to rush into anything like before. Like he said, he has unfinished business." She suddenly brightened. "We could do the modern thing and be friends with benefits, I suppose."

I laughed. We arrived at my office twenty minutes later. We were early; I didn't see Jay's SUV or a truck out front. I waited until my mother and Arnie joined us at the entrance before I punched in the security number that unlocked the glass doors after hours and on weekends.

"Arnie, would you grab that brick behind the hedges?" I asked. "I want to prop the door open so Jay won't have trouble getting in when he arrives."

He reached for the brick and put it in place. We stepped inside the lobby, headed for the elevator, and I pushed the button to the fourth floor. "I hope my landlord didn't renege on his promise to paint and install new carpet," I said.

The bell dinged on the elevator, and we stepped out on my floor and headed toward my office. I slipped my key into the lock and pushed open the door. It was dark inside. "Hold on a minute while I turn on the lights."

I flipped them on.

"Surprise!"

I almost jumped out of my skin at the room filled with people. Flash lights blinked in my face as Jeff snapped pictures.

Mona threw her arms around me. "I wish you could see the look on your face!" she said.

I shook my head as if to clear it. I saw Jay standing behind Mona, along with a couple of men I recognized from the fire department. He gave me a warm smile. Beside him, Elizabeth Larkin, her hair now a flattering reddish brown, winked at me. I was immensely relieved to see her looking so healthy. "What's going on?" I asked.

"We decided to throw a party to celebrate your new office," Mona said. "Elizabeth and I spent all day yesterday picking out new furniture."

I gazed about the room, stunned by the changes. An overstuffed sofa and two chairs in a rich chocolate adorned the newly painted reception room. Plump pillows in an array of fall colors brightened the area, and a distressed coffee table held the latest magazines. The lamps, wall art, and decorative objects tied it all together and gave the room a sophisticated flair.

"Do you like it?" Mona asked. "Elizabeth and I wanted it to be perfect."

"It's gorgeous," I said.

"Wait till you see the rest." She led me into my office where a mahogany desk and matching credenza shared space with other tasteful furniture.

"How did you manage to do all of this so quickly?" I asked.

"We would not have been able to pull it off had everyone not done their part," Mona said.

Someone tapped me on the shoulder. A smiling Liam handed me a glass of champagne.

"Congratulations, Kate," he said and kissed me on the cheek.

I was so touched that I had to fight back tears. "I don't know what to say."

My mother leaned close and whispered in my ear. "Just say thank you."

"Yes, thank you," I managed.

The door opened and Thad stepped inside holding a potted plant. He looked uncomfortable. "Mona told me she was throwing a little party for you," he said, "so I brought you this." He glanced around the room. "Nice office."

I took the plant. "Thank you, Thad," I said, albeit a bit formally since I hadn't completely forgiven him. I knew I'd get over it eventually, and we'd find another reason to disagree. Mona handed him a glass of champagne.

"I don't know if you've met everyone," I said. I

introduced Jeff and they shook hands. Finally, I presented Elizabeth. I had the pleasure of seeing Thad blush. "You look fabulous," he told her.

"Thank you, Dr. Glazer."

Jay pulled me aside. I noticed he was holding a soft drink. "I'm really happy about your new office, Katie," he said, "but the guys and I need to get back to the station."

I smiled at the two men next to Jay. "I can't thank you enough," I said, getting used to the words. They shook my hand, congratulated me, and started for the door.

I followed Jay into the hallway as the other men pushed the button to the elevator.

"Um, Jay?"

He looked at me, and I noted the deep lines of fatigue on his face.

"Do you still want to meet with Evelyn Hunt tomorrow?"

He raked his fingers through his hair. "I forgot about that." The elevator opened. "I'd like to hold off for now," he said. "I've sort of got my hands full."

The elevator doors opened, and they stepped inside. I waited until the doors closed before going back into my office. Even though I felt discouraged that Jay would not make the next appointment with Evelyn, I understood his reasons.

For the next hour, we sipped champagne and sampled Arnie's hors d'oeuvres. I suspected I would put on five pounds before the day was over. Several people from the other offices stopped by, including the bank president and the attorney who'd come to my rescue.

Jeff pulled me aside a few minutes later. "I have to go," he said. "I'm meeting someone at my office to discuss a partnership."

"That's good news!" I said.

He smiled. "Look, I sort of cleared the air with Mona when she called to invite me to your party," he said, keeping his voice down. "I'm hoping she and I can be friends."

"Me too," I said, "since the two of you are my favorite people."

He gave me a quick hug before leaving.

Although I'd had a lot of fun, I was glad when the party started breaking up. I'd eaten so much that all I wanted to do was go home, put on my pajamas, and think about my new office. My mother and aunt cleared away the paper plates while Arnie covered the leftovers.

Finally, it was just Mona and me. "I think it went well," she said.

"I can't believe you pulled it off."

She smiled. "Everybody parked behind the building."

"You bought the furniture?"

"Elizabeth paid half. She's filthy rich like me. She also came up with a great idea on how I could make a real difference in this town. She got so excited thinking about it that she plans to join in. We're going to raise money to build boys and girls clubs in a number of neighborhoods. We're also going to donate money to the police department so they can hire extra personnel. Our goal is to stamp out gang activity."

"That's wonderful!" I said.

"Elizabeth knows the governor, and he's behind us. Also, I came really close to sleeping with the mayor right after Mr. Moneybags died. I think I can convince him to help."

I laughed. "You're something else, Mona," I said, "which is why I love you."

"I love you, too, Kate."

chapter 15

....

I arrived at my office early the next morning so I could move my files from the old cabinet to the new credenza behind my desk. I walked through the rooms that had been freshly painted, carpeted, and filled with tasteful furnishings, and I had an urge to pinch myself to see if I was dreaming.

It was sort of intimidating to be surrounded by such luxury. My patients were going to expect me to be a better psychologist. I was going to have to read more trade journals and sign up for at least one conference each year.

I opened the bottom drawer in my desk and reached for a notepad advertising Zoloft so I could jot down my ideas. Drug salespeople left Thad tons of such pads, not to mention pens, and he passed them on to me, not questioning that I insisted on taking an even number when he offered them. I also had exactly thirty-six pens in my stash. While I realized that number was divisible by three, an odd number, I found comfort in knowing it could be divided by two as well. I suddenly realized that if I stopped talking to Thad for good, I would lose out on the freebies.

Mona arrived as I was sitting at my desk enjoying a cup of coffee. She came in and sat on my new sofa. I could tell something was wrong.

"Bad news," she said. "There was a shooting in Ricky Perez's neighborhood late last night. A member of a gang called the Bloods was killed in a drive-by. The police suspect the shooter is someone from the Thirty-Eight Specials. They're the ones who recently moved into Ricky's neighborhood. Mrs. Perez said Ricky hasn't eaten or slept in two days. She thinks he knows something, but he isn't talking."

"He probably does," I said, "seeing how the baseball bat had his fingerprints all over it."

"Police questioned him about the bat. He told them it was his bat, but that he hadn't seen it in a while."

"That's convenient," I said.

"Do you think he did it?"

"Like I said, the evidence is incriminating as hell."

"Mrs. Perez and her daughter swear he is being framed. His mother kept him home from school today, but she couldn't get off work so he's with Mrs. Perez. She asked me to see if you could talk to Ricky."

I hesitated. I wasn't so sure of Ricky's innocence. "How is Father Demarco?"

"He's still critical, but he's going to be okay. Police were finally able to question him late yesterday. He claims he never saw his attacker, and he did not open the door for anyone that morning. He thinks whoever did it was hiding in the church, just waiting. Father Demarco suspects the person who assaulted him was from the Thirty-Eight Specials because he was making trouble for them. He pushed for his congregation to band to-gether and help him take action against gang violence."

"Father Demarco sounds like a brave man," I said.

"Yes, but look what happened. The police depart-ments in this city need more staff, and they need per-sonnel who are knowledgeable about gangs. That's where Elizabeth and I come in."

"I'd say you found your cause," I told her.

She nodded. "Oh, and get this," she said. "Elizabeth has this hunky bodyguard. I'm thinking I should get one, too."

I arched one brow. "Do you feel like your life is in danger?"

Mona grinned. "No, but I could pretend. I could cut words from a newspaper and mail menacing notes to myself."

We both laughed.

"Will you at least talk to Ricky?"

"For you? Yes."

Evelyn Hunt led me into her office and invited me to sit down. "I'm sorry Jay couldn't make it," she said, "but I've read about the fires in the newspapers. How are you handling it?"

"It's not easy, but what can I do? It doesn't make sense that someone would target firefighters. I suppose the answer to your question is that I take it one day at a time." Finally, I told her about Mandy.

"Do you think Jay is cheating?" she asked.

"I don't think so, but they say the wife is the last one to know."

"Have you accused him?"

"I've hinted at it."

She looked thoughtful. "Do you know other firefighters' wives?" she asked. "Someone you could talk to who shares your concerns about her husband's safety?"

"I sort of backed off from those relationships after Jay and I separated," I said. "But I know the wives talk among themselves and offer each other support."

"Perhaps you should renew some of your old friendships," she said.

"It isn't easy for me to talk to the wives. I know some of them struggle with being married to a firefighter, so I hate to confess my fears and add to their burden."

"Who *do* you talk to?" Evelyn asked.

I told her about Mona.

"But your friend Mona isn't married to a firefighter," Evelyn said, "so she isn't going to know what it feels like. If you had a small support system in place, you would be able to talk to somebody who *does* know what it feels like."

"I'll think about it."

I was still pondering Evelyn Hunt's words when I arrived at my office, where Mrs. Perez and Ricky were waiting. Mrs. Perez made a small fuss over the new decor, but I could tell she had more on her mind than my fancy furniture. I invited Ricky into my office and closed the door.

He was dressed in jeans and an Atlanta Falcons jersey with the number nineteen on it. "I didn't know you were an Atlanta Falcons fan."

He nodded. "Yeah."

"Which player is number nineteen?" I asked.

"What?" He blinked at me.

"You're wearing number nineteen," I pointed out.

He shifted on the sofa and avoided eye contact. "I don't remember. I guess I have a lot on my mind."

"I heard about the baseball bat, Ricky."

His eyes flitted about the room. "The police act like it is some big deal that my fingerprints were on it," he said. "I told them it was *my* bat. My grandfather bought it for me when I was in Little League. Of course it would have my prints on it."

"But it doesn't explain why it was at the site where a priest was beaten, does it?"

"I don't know how the bat ended up there," he said.

"I haven't played baseball since I was maybe fourteen. I could have lent it to somebody. I don't remember."

"Your grandfather bought you a special bat, and you don't know what happened to it?"

He gave me an odd look. "Who said it was special? It was just a regular baseball bat like you can buy any-where."

"I figured it was special because your grandfather bought it for you."

His eyes filled with tears. "I'm sick of all these questions. You're no different than the police."

"You're not required to answer my questions," I said. "You aren't even required to be here. Why *are* you here, Ricky?"

"Because of my mother and grandmother. And because of my attorney," he added.

"Oh, right. Your attorney wants me to go to court for you. Even if I could, I don't think you'd want me to, because I think you're lying. You're lying about Father Demarco, and you're withholding information about a murder that took place last night in your neighbor-hood."

"You don't know what you're talking about."

"Here's what I know," I said. "I know there was a young man who was an honor student and dreamed of becoming a doctor. I know he got the crap stomped out of him three weeks ago by a gang called the Thirty-Eight Specials. I know there was an old priest who was viciously attacked for making a lot of noise against this gang, and that you were closer to that priest than most people. You would have known how to get in and out of that church, you would have known where to hide, and you would have known when he was most vulnerable."

Ricky buried his face in his hands.

"You're in way over your head, Ricky," I said.

He looked up. "What you don't know is what it's like living in my neighborhood," he said. "Say somebody hurts your mother or your sister or your girlfriend. Are you going to call the police?" He gave a grunt. "The police don't even want to come into our neighborhood."

"So you're saying the guy who was shot to death last night hurt mothers and sisters and girlfriends?"

"I'm saying he may have deserved exactly what he got."

"What did he do to your sister, Ricky?" I asked. I could see that I'd caught Ricky off guard with my question.

We both looked at each other but said nothing.

Finally, Ricky held his head up. "This guy that got shot last night?" he began. "Well, the cops would take him in, and the next thing you know he was back on the street again. And even if a young girl was to go to her parents, which doesn't often happen, do you think she's going to point a finger at a Bloods member in a police lineup or testify against him in court?" he said. "She would know better."

I leaned back in my chair and regarded Ricky, noting the changes in him that had taken place since I last saw him; changes that his family had missed.

"You know what I do when I get really stressed?" I said. He looked at me. "I count things. I do multiplication tables in my head."

"That's weird," Ricky said.

I nodded. "You know what's even weirder?" I asked. "I know how much that jersey you're wearing cost, because I purchased one for my husband a couple of years ago. And you're telling me you have no idea who number nineteen for the Atlanta Falcons is. You're walking around wearing an expensive jersey with the number nineteen plastered on the front and back, and you're clueless about the player."

"So what? Who cares?"

"Nobody," I said, "because the number nineteen means nothing unless you multiply it by two and get thirty-eight. And I'm looking at the guy who plays for Thirty-Eight."

Silence. Ricky stared down at his feet. "They weren't supposed to kill him," he said softly.

I stood and walked to the window that looked out over the parking lot. I did not want Ricky to know how sad and angry and helpless I felt. I was so sad and angry that I wanted to cry. I wanted to kick something. "What about medical school, Ricky?" I asked quietly.

"We don't have a lot of doctors come out of our neighborhood," he said.

I sat in my chair and pulled one of my cards from a plastic holder. I handed it to Ricky. "Call me when you're ready to be the first."

* * *

Eddie Franks wore a sheepish expression as he followed me into my office and sat down. "Your place looks real nice, Doc," he said.

"Thanks, Ed."

He winced. "Please don't call me Ed."

"Don't call me Doc, and I won't call you Ed."

"I know you're mad at me," he said.

I arched one brow. "You think? Did you tell your parole officer that you made arrangements to take a naive, never-been-married woman to Las Vegas to elope?"

"Oh no," he said. "I couldn't possibly tell—"

"But I can," I said and had the pleasure of watching him squirm.

He sat up straight and squared his shoulders. "Dr. Holly," he said, giving me his best smile, "you'll have to agree that, in the end, I did the right thing. I told Trixie the truth. I delivered her home safely, and I apologized to everyone for making them worry."

"*After* my poor mother almost had a nervous breakdown," I said, reaching over and punching him hard in the shoulder.

"Ouch!" His eyes widened. "Are you supposed to hit a patient?"

I hit him again, this time harder. He yelped, rubbed his shoulder, and moved to the other end of the sofa. "You could get into trouble for that, you know."

I looked around. "Gee, I don't see any witnesses, do

you? It's your word against mine, and I've never been in the big house. I could stick my letter opener through your gizzard and get away with it."

He eyed the door.

"Don't even *think* of trying to leave," I said. I crossed my arms. "Where did you take my aunt when you were supposed to be at all-night bowling?"

He looked surprised. "We were at all-night bowling."

I gave him my look.

"I swear!" He stiffened as though preparing himself for another blow. "I never laid a hand on Trixie. I have the utmost respect for her."

"So what are your plans?"

He gave me a blank look. "Other than trying to get out of this office alive?"

"Don't joke with me, Ed."

He winced again. "Please don't call me Ed."

I pulled a book from beneath my chair that my mother had purchased at a flea market when I'd started dating. It had been weathered and dated even then, the pages yellowed and tattered. "I want you to read this book from cover to cover," I said.

Eddie took the book and opened it. Some of the pages fell from it. "*The Etiquette of Dating*?" he read aloud.

"The nineteen fifty-four edition," I said. "It doesn't say anything about keeping a young lady out all night and making her twin sister crazy with worry. It doesn't say one word about having the young lady's niece drive across town at dawn because the stupid guy thought it would be fun to go to Vegas and get married after only a week of knowing each other."

"I didn't go through with it," he said.

"Read the damn book, Eddie. Not once but twice. In the meantime, you're going to take care of all your old business. Then, when I'm convinced that you can act like a gentleman, I might just let you date my aunt." I leaned closer. Eddie leaned away. "Do we understand each other, Ed?"

He winced. "Please don't call me Ed."

"I'll see you next week. Same place, same time."

He looked relieved as he got up and started for the door.

"Ed?"

He turned.

"Try not to do anything else to piss me off."

Lying on my sofa, Alice Smithers listened quietly as I led her to a state of total relaxation. I saw her body go limp and her cheek muscles slack, and I knew she had gone into trance successfully.

"Alice, I'd like you to remember a time when you were a little girl and you felt very safe," I said. I waited. "Can you remember?"

The woman on the sofa nodded, but it was not a woman's voice I heard. "Yeth."

"Where are you?"

"With my daddy. We are at a fair. I am riding a horsey. It goes round and round."

"A carousel horse?"

"Yeth. My daddy is standing by me. He wants to make sure I don't fall." She sniffed the air.

"What do you smell?"

"Cotton candy. My daddy bought me a big bag." She giggles. "It's sticky."

"Is there anyone else with you?" I asked.

"My granny. She tells Daddy the cotton candy will spoil my dinner, but he laughs."

"Where is your mother?"

Alice frowned. "I don't have one of those. Just Daddy and Granny."

"Where are you living?"

"We live in a small white house and grow beans and tomatoes and corn in our garden. I help Granny pull the bad stuff."

"Bad stuff?"

"Weeds. Weeds are bad. They choke the beans and tomatoes and corn. Weeds hurt them."

"How old are you, Alice?"

"Four."

"Okay, let's move ahead in time. You're five years old now. Can you tell me where you are?"

Alice frowns. "I don't know this place."

"What does it look like?"

"Dark." She started to cry.

"Take my hand, Alice," I said. I reached for her

234

hand and held it. "You don't have to be in that dark place by yourself."

"I can't see anything," she said, gulping back tears. "There is a door."

"Can you open it?"

"No." She started to cry. "I can't get out."

"Where is your daddy?"

"I don't know. He and Granny got lost at the fair."

"How did they get lost?"

"They got lost after I rode the horsey that went round and round."

"But you must've seen where they were before they got lost."

"They were on this big wheel that went high in the sky."

"A Ferris wheel?"

"Yeth."

"Where were you?"

She spoke quickly. "On a bench watching them. I did not want to ride the big wheel. I was watching them go round and round and round and—" She suddenly stopped talking. "Oh no," she said. "No, I don't want to."

Alice's body went rigid. I studied her closely, wanting to learn as much as I could but prepared to stop everything if she became too distressed.

"No, I don't want to," the little girl voice repeated, whining.

"Who are you talking to, Alice?"

"This lady is saying I have to come with her, but I

tell her I'm supposed to sit on the bench and wait for my daddy." Alice started sobbing. She squeezed my hand until it hurt.

Alice had returned to her four-year-old self at the fair, and I assumed she was being abducted by her mother, Carmen. I wondered if we should keep going. "Take a deep breath, Alice," I said, my tone gentle but authoritative as I tried to guide her safely. "You're standing in front of the ocean, and the breeze is blowing through your hair."

She immediately relaxed, and her grip loosened.

"Okay, Alice, I want you to go back to watching the Ferris wheel, and when the lady comes up to you I want you to keep holding my hand and try to hold on to feeling very safe with me. And while you see the scene, imagine you are watching it on TV. You can turn the volume up or down, and you can turn your feelings up or down too, okay?"

I waited. "Is she there?"

"Yeth."

"Who is the lady, Alice?"

She frowned. "I saw her before, but I don't remember when. I think I saw her with Daddy one time. She might be my mother. I don't want to go with her, but she picks me up and tells me I must be polite because she is all grown up and I'm not. And she puts me in a car that I have not seen before. And then I start crying and . . . Ouch!" Alice reeled.

"What happened?"

"She slapped me! My whole face stings, and I'm

236

crying louder. I don't like the way she looks and smells and I don't like the dark place. The dark place is like weeds. It chokes me and I feel like a green bean or a tomato that is dying. And I hear these noises in the walls, and I can feel something crawling over my legs, and—" Alice screamed and screamed and tried to jerk her hand free.

"Alice," I said, trying to talk over the screaming and twitching. "You're back at the beach with the wind and surf. I'm holding your hand."

She stopped screaming.

"I'm going to count to three and you're going to wake up, but you're still going to be a little girl."

When Alice opened her eyes, I was holding Bubba Bear, the stuffed animal that was well loved by my young patients. I noted her look of excitement, and I introduced her to him. I got up and sat on the sofa beside her. "Would you like to hold him?"

She reached out, and I placed the soft bear in her arms. We sat there quietly. From time to time, I took her hand and squeezed it gently, and I continued to sit there as she sank against me, still holding Bubba Bear.

I was getting ready to leave for the day when Mona peeked inside my office. "Lewis Barnes is on the line," she said. I could see the worry on her face, but, despite being best friends, I couldn't discuss the session I'd had with Ricky. I didn't have to tell Mona it wasn't good; she knew me well enough.

I stared at the phone and felt a dull ache inside. Nobody liked to think of a kid's life going down the toilet.

"Aren't you going to answer it?" Mona asked.

I picked up the phone, and she closed the door. "Hello, Mr. Barnes," I said, using what Mona called my professional voice.

"I've got Ricky in my office," he said. "We've been discussing his case."

"Mr. Barnes, I don't know what you expect from me, but I have not agreed to get involved in Ricky Perez's legal matters. I'm not a forensic psychologist."

"I know that, Dr. Holly. That's not why I'm calling. Ricky would like to speak with you."

I felt a quiver of anxiety as I waited.

"Dr. Holly?"

"Yes, Ricky?"

"I, um, just told Mr. Barnes everything," he said in a halting voice. "I'm sorry I lied to you. I was scared."

I heard his voice catch, heard him sniff. "I know."

"I hit Father Demarco with the baseball bat," he said. He choked back a sob. "I never wanted to hurt him. But I was so angry. I wanted that Blood member to pay for what he did to girls, and I was willing to make any kind of deal. So I linked up with the Thirty-Eights. I'm sorry I lied to you."

I swallowed. "How can I help you, Ricky?"

He started crying. "You already have," he said between tears. "I never would have been able to tell my mom and my grandmother if you hadn't called me down. I just want you to promise not to give up on me, because I want to be able to talk to you some more."

"I'm never going to give up on you, Ricky," I said, my voice wavering. Screw professional detachment, I thought. I'd have to be made out of stone not to feel something for the kid on the other end of the line. "You're going to be the first doctor to come out of your neighborhood," I reminded him. I had no grand illusions, only hope.

chapter 16

························

After hanging up, I sat at my desk and tried to gather my thoughts. Mona was right. I had a crappy job. She knocked on my door. Her expression was troubled. "Mrs. Perez just called. I guess you know what it was about."

"How are they taking it?"

"Not so good. But Lewis Barnes said Ricky won't do hard time since he will be tried in juvenile court. He might spend time in the juvenile detention center."

"How is he going to get out of the gang alive?"

Mona sighed. "That's the tricky part. Both Mrs. Perez and Ricky's mother are prepared to leave at a moment's notice with the clothes on their backs. Lewis and I are working on a plan in case they have to do that. In the meantime, he is going to talk to the judge. Ricky will have what the gang refers to as 'street cred' by being locked up, which is the safest place for him right now anyway."

"Did he say anything about the shooting?" I asked.

"No, but the police told Barnes the so-called 'Blood' member ate a bullet for honing in on the Thirty-Eights' territory. The penalty for that is death. It had nothing to do with Ricky." Mona sighed. "It's going to take someone smarter than Elizabeth and me to figure out a way to curtail gang violence, but there are supposedly experts who stay on top of that sort of thing."

I was relieved that Ricky had no involvement with the gang member's killing. I knew that even though he would confess to beating Father Demarco, he would never mention the Thirty-Eights or the deal he'd made. Ricky would protect his sister no matter what.

"How is Elizabeth, by the way?" I asked.

"She took out a restraining order against her husband and that crackpot doctor; plus, she's got that stud of a bodyguard."

"I'm glad you discussed your desire to raise funds for the boys and girls clubs," I said. "It will help divert her attention."

Mona nodded. "Um."

"Um, what?"

"I sort of agreed to be Jeff's friend if he swore never to tell anyone that I tried to seduce him."

"Jeff is a big boy. He'll live."

"Um. Do you think your mom or aunt or Arnie will say anything?"

"My aunt doesn't gossip and Arnie pretty much

minds his own business. But in high school, my mother was voted the girl least likely to keep a secret."

Mona slapped a hand over her eyes. "I'm screwed."

I was tired when I arrived home at the end of the day. While I'd made progress with Alice Smithers, I was still concerned over Ricky Perez and feeling bad for his family. I worried that his sister would not get the help she needed, that Ricky would never recover emotionally from what he'd done, that his mother and Mrs. Perez might spend years living with the shame of his crime. Of course, if it were up to me the whole world would be in therapy, just like the orthodontist who thinks everyone needs braces.

Mike greeted me happily at the door, and I scooped her up and twirled around. Her tail wagged at warp speed; I was thrilled to have the old Mike back.

The phone rang. I put Mike down and answered. It was Jeff.

"Guess what? I have a new partner."

"Fantastic!"

"I would never have gotten around to advertising for one if you hadn't bitched, moaned, and nagged."

I smiled. "Why, thank you, Jeff. I'm touched."

I checked my other messages. Jay had called and promised to call back. Ricky's tearful mother left a message, thanking me for helping her son and wanting to know if I would consider seeing him while he was in juvenile detention. I made a mental note to call her back.

The machine beeped and Bitsy Stout spoke. "Kate Holly, guess what I found in my yard when I returned from my Bible study meeting? Dog poop, that's what. This is the last time I'm going to warn you to stop letting that, um, dog of yours poop in my yard." She hung up.

At least she hadn't called Mike ugly.

When my doorbell rang, I was surprised to find Jay standing there, wearing a weary smile. "What are you doing here?" I asked as he stepped inside. Mike raced toward him and put her paws on his legs.

"You got a hug for a tired fireman?" he asked, reaching down to rub Mike's head.

I slipped my arms around him, and we held each other tightly, saying nothing, just enjoying the contact. I caught the smell of soap, mingled with sweat and soot. I stepped back and noted the deep lines of fatigue on his face. "Are you okay?"

"I am now," he said. He leaned down and kissed me. It was long and lingering, and I felt it reach down far and warm my soul. He raised his head and smiled. "I was hoping I could grab a shower if you have any guy soap on hand. It'll ruin my macho image if I go back to the station smelling like magnolia blossoms."

"Gee, I don't know," I said. "You might have to bathe in Mike's flea dip."

"Silly woman. Maybe I could crash here if the sofa isn't already taken." He glanced past me.

"Silly man," I said, closing the door behind him. "Have you eaten?"

"I grabbed something earlier."

I took his hand and led him upstairs. I kept his stash of underwear and socks in one of the dresser drawers. I opened it and pulled out what he would need, plus a pair of old sweats. While he undressed, I reached inside my closet and grabbed his jeans and a long-sleeved shirt so they would be there for him later. "I hope this is okay," I said.

He barely glanced at it. "Thanks." He wadded up his clothes and put them on the floor beside his shoes. "I hope the water is hot," he said, walking naked into the bathroom.

I stared at his broad back and trim hips and gave a soft sigh of feminine pleasure. "Me, too," I said.

I hurried downstairs, heated a couple of cans of soup, and made grilled cheese sandwiches. The phone rang. I felt a cold knot in my stomach when I saw the caller ID readout. I recognized the area code from before.

I answered.

"This is Mandy."

"What can I do for you, Mandy?"

"I need to speak to Jay. I haven't been able to reach him on his cell phone."

"That's strange," I said, "because I can."

Silence at first. "It's important."

"He's in the shower. I'll be happy to take a message."

"You have no right to keep me from talking to him," she said. "Don't you *get it*? He's not your husband anymore."

I could almost feel her hostility burning through the phone line. "I don't think *you* get it, Mandy," I said, more calmly than I felt. "This is where Jay sleeps at night, and if he hasn't called you back by now it's not likely he will."

I heard a deep intake of breath, followed by a dial tone.

Jay walked into the kitchen as I put the food on the table. He wore his sweats but was bare from the waist up. I liked him that way. He sat down at the table. "Would you like a beer?"

"No, thanks. I don't know if I'll get a call. How about a soda instead?" he asked.

"Sure." I didn't ask questions.

He picked up one of the sandwiches and looked at me. "Thanks, babe."

I smiled. I knew he wasn't thanking me for the sandwich. He was relieved that I wasn't pushing for information or making demands as I would have done in the past.

We decided to crash early. Jay put his radio and pager on the night table beside him, pulled off his sweats, and climbed beneath the covers. "Come here," he said, reaching out.

I stripped down to my panties, turned off the lamp, and climbed in beside him. He pulled me flush against his body, his broad chest warm on my back. "This sure beats the hell out of sleeping on a cot," he said, a smile in his voice.

I felt the tension melt from him. His breath was

warm on the back of my neck as he settled into sleep.
The rise and fall of his chest lulled me, and I felt myself drift, enveloped in all that was Jay.

It was times such as these, when we pushed life's
many complexities aside and focused on simple human
needs, that Jay and I were at our best.

I wasn't sure how long I had slept before I heard the
alarm go off on Jay's radio. I felt him climb from the
bed, heard him slip on his clothes. As always, I felt a
sense of dread, only this time it was worse because I
knew the alarm only sounded when a fire was bad and
extra manpower was needed.

I turned over. "What time is it?"

"Early. Go back to sleep."

I pushed the button on my wristwatch. The face lit
up. Two thirty a.m. I swallowed hard. "Do you
think—"

"Don't, Katie."

I tried to make my voice steady. "Please call me as
soon as you can."

He planted a quick kiss on my head and raced down
the stairs. A moment later, I heard him pull from the
driveway.

I knew I wouldn't be able to go back to sleep.

Wearing my warmest robe and sitting at the kitchen
table, I fretted through my first and second cups of
coffee. I watched the clock. Mike sat at my feet, still as
a statue. I reached down and stroked her ear. My shoulders felt weighted with worry. I crossed my arms on
the kitchen table and laid my head down.

I was jolted awake by the sound of a car door slamming outside. It was after four a.m. I almost toppled the chair as I ran to the front door. I threw it open.

Carter Atkins stood on the other side.

"What are you doing here?" I demanded, angry to find him there instead of Jay.

He swallowed so hard that his Adam's apple bobbed along his throat. "Jay has been hurt. He was taken away in an ambulance."

"You're lying!" Adrenaline rushed through my body. I swayed. Carter reached out, but I slapped his hand away. I tried to close the door; he stuck his foot in it. Fear clutched at my throat. How many times had Jay warned me to stay away from him?

"Go away!" I yelled. "I know what you did. You tried to make Ronnie Sumner look guilty, but you were the one setting those fires."

"No, I—"

"You're angry because you can't pass the exam." I shoved the door harder. "You hate firefighters because you know you'll never be one."

"Kate, listen to me."

"No!" I glared at him. "If you don't leave this minute, I'll scream so loud the whole neighborhood will hear me."

"I'm telling the truth. I heard it over the scanner, and I didn't think you'd be in any condition to drive so I came to get you."

"I'm not going anywhere with you!"

"You don't *have* to ride with me," he said. "I'll

follow you to the hospital in my truck." He pulled his
foot from the door. "I'll wait for you or I'll leave. Tell
me now."

He'd backed away from the door, leaving me free to
close it. I struggled with my emotions. If I trusted him,
then I would have to believe Jay was really hurt. "Why
have you been hanging around me?" I said.

He looked down at his feet. "Because you don't
treat me like I'm a retard. Because I care what happens
to Jay even if he hates me."

He appeared genuinely concerned. My eyes spurted
tears. "Don't you lie to me, Carter," I said, shocked at
the sound of my own voice. "Don't you dare lie to
me."

A single tear slid down one of his cheeks. "Jay and
three other men fell through the first floor of a house
and into the basement. They ran out of oxygen before
they could be pulled safely out."

I didn't want to believe him. "How bad?"

"They're alive. Call the hospital if you like."

I closed the door, locked it, and hurried to the phone.
I fumbled through the phone book, my fingers numb
as I searched for the telephone number to the local
hospital. I dialed the number to the ER and explained
to the woman on the other end who I was.

"Yes, we have a Jay Rush listed," she said, "but I'm
not allowed to give out information over the telephone."

"I'm his wife!" I repeated. "Just tell me if he's
alive."

"Yes."

I hung up and ran to the door with Mike on my heels. I opened it to find Carter sitting on my front steps. He stood. "I can be dressed in three minutes," I said.

I turned so quickly my head spun. I raced upstairs, Mike right behind me. I flipped on the light switch, tore off my robe, and grabbed my jeans from the chair where I'd left them. My hands shook. I could barely hold the waist band open to push my legs through.

I searched for my sneakers. I dropped one of them twice before I could put it on. My fingers were clumsy as I tried tying the laces, and I couldn't stop crying. I took the stairs one at a time because I feared my knees might fold at any moment. I reached the kitchen. I was not prepared for what I saw.

Carter stood in my kitchen. Behind him, Mandy Mason held a pistol to his head. She wore thin latex gloves. I opened my mouth to speak but nothing came out.

"You don't look happy to see me, Kate," she said.

I gulped. "What are you doing?" I cried. I saw resignation in Carter's eyes. He was a man waiting to die.

"Have you ever heard of payback?" she asked calmly.

"I don't know what you're talking about."

"C'mon, Kate, you had to know your husband was screwing my brains out. Everybody at the station knew. Excuse me, I mean your ex-husband."

"I don't believe you."

"Denial is a good thing," she said. "Why is the wife always the last to know?" She smiled. "Why don't you ask me where Jay's birthmark is?" she said.

I suddenly knew with all my heart that Jay had not been unfaithful. "Why are you telling me this?"

"Because I want you to hurt like I was hurt," she said. "I want you to experience the humiliation that I went through when Jay finished with me. When he tossed me aside as though I was nothing," she added.

"She's lying," Carter said.

"Shut up!" she yelled. She hit him in the head with the butt of the pistol. He staggered forward. I started toward him and saw something from the corner of my eye at the window over my kitchen sink. Someone was out there. I averted my gaze quickly.

"Come any closer, and he's dead," Mandy said. Mike growled.

I could almost feel the hatred roiling inside the woman. "You're going to shoot us?" I asked. "My neighbors will call the police the minute they hear the shots."

"Perhaps you'd rather burn like the others."

I frowned. I saw the look of disbelief in Carter's eyes. Realization hit me like a brick. "You started the fires?"

"I tried so hard to be the best firefighter I could, but it was never enough. Not for a man like my father, who had walked right into the belly of a fire. A man who became a hero to each and all, even though it almost cost him his life," she said. "I wanted to be just like him, but there was only one hero in our home and it wasn't me. I was nothing."

Bitter tears streamed down her face. "The men at the fire station in West Virginia liked me, and I enjoyed being liked by them. I enjoyed being special." Her bottom lip quivered. "But men talk, you know? They gossip. My father called me a whore." She shook her head. "I couldn't have that. I decided those men would have to pay, not only for their sins but for my father's as well." She laughed bitterly. "They never suspected that I was behind the fire that snuffed out three of their own."

I could tell Carter was as stunned as I was. "What does that have to do with Jay and his men?" I asked.

"My father asked Jay to hire me because he wanted me out of the way. I embarrassed him. I was angry at first. But then I met Jay, and he was different. He treated me like I was *somebody*. We could have had something if it weren't for you. But in the end, he was no different from the rest." She shrugged. "I wanted him to pay. I wanted to make the men who watched him make a fool out of me pay."

I stared into her eyes as she continued on. I recognized the wild, disjointed expression because I had seen it in the psychiatric ward at the hospital. I was familiar with the ramblings of a mind that had lost all direction.

Still holding the gun to Carter's head, Mandy

reached for the knobs on my gas stove and began turning them on.

Carter clasped his hands together in front of him and made a large fist.

I could already smell the gas coming from the stove. "You weren't even in town when some of those fires were set," I said, trying to distract her even though I had figured it out. "You were calling from a different area code."

"Dumb bitch. I was calling from the cell phone I got in West Virginia. I never left Atlanta."

I suddenly leaned over the sink, pretending to heave. "Please turn off the gas!" I cried. "It's making me sick." If someone was outside I wanted them to know that my kitchen was filling with toxic fumes.

Mandy pulled out an old butane lighter, and fear ripped through my heart. "Come here," she said, her voice deadly calm.

I hesitated. She pointed the gun at me. I stepped forward, and, without warning, the window over my sink shattered. Startled, Mandy fired the pistol at me, and I felt the bullet graze my shoulder. Mike lunged at her, snatching Mandy's attention for a second. She aimed the gun at Mike, and I screamed. Carter swung his fists around and hit Mandy in the temple. She sank to her knees, dropping the pistol. The lighter skidded across the floor. Carter dived toward the pistol as Mandy crawled toward the lighter. Her hand was within an inch of it; I only had a heartbeat to kick it out of her grasp. I was too late. She picked it up, flipped open the top, and smiled.

Then Carter fired the pistol. Her face registered shock and bewilderment. I kicked, and my foot hit her wrist. The lighter flew from her hands, and I fell on it, fumbling to close the top. Carter turned off the gas.

The front door burst open, and I saw two policemen rush in; both of them had their weapons drawn. Mike went into a fit of barking.

"Put the gun on the floor!" one of the cops yelled. Carter did as he was told. "Both of you, face down on the floor, hands behind your back!" he yelled several times. "Now!"

Carter and I hit the floor. We were immediately cuffed and frisked for weapons. One of the officers checked the knobs on the stove, unlocked the kitchen door and threw it open, obviously to clear the fumes. The other officer checked a bleeding Mandy.

"I can explain," I said.

The absolute last person I expected to see standing in front of my house was Bitsy Stout.

"What are you doing out here?" I asked, rubbing my wrists where the handcuffs had been. A paramedic was treating my shoulder, and I winced as he cleaned the wound and covered it with a bandage. Another paramedic was examining Carter's head. Mandy had already been taken away in an ambulance.

Bitsy didn't quite meet my gaze. "I just saved your life," she said. "Me and my pellet gun," she added.

"You were the one outside my kitchen window? How did you know?"

"Your house was lit up, and I heard yelling. I ran home, dialed nine-one-one, and grabbed my gun."

"Dammit!" one of the cops said. "I just stepped in dog shit."

"I should be going," Bitsy said.

I stared in disbelief. "You were putting dog poop in my front yard?" I asked her.

"I was returning it," she said indignantly.

"My dog has not been pooping in your yard!" I shouted. "She can't get out of the fence to poop in *anybody's* yard."

"Oh," Bitsy said, seemingly embarrassed. "Well then, what's important is to remember that I saved your life." She hurried across the street.

One of the officers stepped up to me. "I just got word from the hospital. Your husband is in guarded condition. His injuries are not life threatening," he said.

Tears of relief filled my eyes.

At the hospital, I was led to Jay's room. A tube of oxygen had been inserted in his nose and an IV needle was taped to one hand. Both his head and chest were bandaged. Although someone obviously had tried to clean him up, his face was still streaked with soot.

A doctor stepped inside the room. "Mrs. Rush?"

I turned. He must've seen the panic in my eyes.

"Your husband is going to be okay. He was treated for smoke inhalation. He has a concussion, several cracked ribs, and a broken ankle. We've given him something for pain, so he's probably going to sleep for a while."

Fresh tears filled my eyes. "Do you know the condition of the other men?"

"They're pretty banged up. One was airlifted to the burn center."

My mother came into the room and gasped at the sight of my bloodstained sweater. I'd called her from the ambulance and briefed her. She blinked several times. "What in the H-E-L-L happened to you?" she demanded.

"It's complicated, Mom," I said.

Once I'd been taken to another room and examined, Aunt Trixie and Arnie joined my mother and me. Arnie was in full makeup. He wore a three-piece suit that glittered. I told them what had occurred. "I have to be with Jay," I said.

"You don't want him to see you like that," my mother said, motioning at my stained sweater. "And your face is a mess."

"Help her out of her blouse," Arnie said, as he slipped off his jacket and pulled off his tank top. He opened the small satchel he carried with him at all times. My mother wet a paper towel at the sink and wiped my face and neck.

By the time Arnie finished with me, I was wearing his tank top and makeup. I returned to Jay's room, where I stood beside his bed for more than an hour before he opened his eyes. He gave me an odd look. "Have you been at a party?" he asked, his voice groggy.

"It's a long story," I said.

"I fell through a floor."

"I heard." I squeezed his hand. "You're going to be okay, though."

"What about the others?"

"They're alive."

"I need to tell you about Mandy. I've been looking into her past. I should have told you."

I saw he was getting anxious. "You have to rest, Jay."

"I got a call from her father on the way to the fire last night. He heard about the suspicious fires we were having. She's still in Atlanta, but I don't know where. She's dangerous, Kate. She—"

"We already know."

"Carter didn't do it."

"Everything is under control, Jay," I said. "Mandy isn't going to hurt anyone else."

His questioning gaze met mine.

"It's over for her," I said.

Finally, he closed his eyes and drifted off.

I was sitting by the bed holding Jay's hand when Carter peeked in. "How is he?" he whispered.

"He's banged up, but it could have been worse. How about you?" I asked.

"I've got a lump on my head, but the X-ray was okay, so I'm good." He motioned to my shoulder.

"Superficial wound," I said, repeating what the doctor had told me.

"Mandy's not doing so well," he said. "The bullet went into her chest. She's in surgery. I feel bad that I had to shoot her. I've never shot anyone before. I've never even held a gun."

"It was either her or us," I reminded him.

"She lied, Kate. The reason she knew where Jay's birthmark was is because she climbed in the shower with him one night. Uninvited," he added.

"I don't need an explanation, Carter. Some things you just know in your heart." I felt guilty for ever doubting Jay. I knew it was my own fault he didn't share as much. He never knew if I was going to go off the deep end.

He looked down. "I didn't know she was the one setting those fires. I never should have accused—"

"Stop it."

He nodded. "I have to get home. My mother needs me."

"We'll talk soon," I said.

My mom entered the room a few minutes later, carrying a cardboard cup. "I figured you could use some coffee," she said, offering it to me.

"Thanks, Mom." I sipped cautiously.

"I called Mona. She's on her way."

I wasn't sure what Mona could do, but I liked knowing she'd be there. "Thank you."

She looked at Jay, who was still out. "He's going to be okay, honey," she said. "It's going to take time for him to get back on his feet. He's going to need someone to look after him."

"I'll take him home with me," I said. "I may have to rent a hospital bed for downstairs."

"Trixie, Arnell, and I will help you, of course."

I almost smiled. It was too soon to start dreading it. "I know."

"What about you?" she asked.

"I'm perfectly fine," I insisted. I knew I could always fall apart later if I had to.

She left the room.

I sipped my coffee and gazed out the window where dawn had already announced a new day. Mona came and went. Sometime later, Jay stirred and opened his eyes, then looked straight at me. I saw the love.

I leaned over and very gently pressed my lips to his forehead. I felt his body relax as sleep and good drugs found him once more.

Keep reading for a special preview
of Charlotte Hughes's next novel,

HANGING BY
A THREAD

Coming soon from Jove Books!

"I don't like the looks of this, Kate," Mona said, her binoculars trained on the back parking lot of St. Francis Catholic Church, where people were pulling in and getting out of their vehicles. "They all look pissed off."

Mona and I were parked across the street from the church. The neighborhood was low-income, and Mona's Jaguar didn't exactly blend. Mona was probably the only receptionist in Atlanta who owned a Jag, but her late husband had been filthy stinking rich.

"Of course they're pissed off," I said. "That's why they're in anger management. By the way, why do you keep binoculars in your car?"

"Don't ask," Mona said.

I shrugged. I didn't really care one way or the other. I was busy dealing with a light case of anger myself.

After spending six weeks caring for my firefighter ex-husband, who'd been injured by a nutso arsonist, we had planned to celebrate his full recovery that evening. A steak dinner at our favorite restaurant, followed by lots of hot sex at my place.

That is, until I'd gotten the call from a colleague I barely knew, asking me to cover the last meeting of her anger management group. A family emergency, a frantic Ruth Melvin had said when she called from her cell phone. She was at the Atlanta airport waiting to catch the next plane to Chicago. I was the third person she'd called. I was her last resort.

I had begrudgingly agreed to do it. I figured I could cut the meeting short and still meet Jay for dinner at eight o'clock. We could eat quickly and be home shortly after nine. There was still hope.

What I had not counted on was Mona Epps—my best friend, who also worked in my office for free—getting all paranoid on me. She had insisted on going with me.

I checked my wristwatch. "I need to get over there," I said. "The meeting starts at six thirty."

"I still don't like it," Mona said, handing me her binoculars. "What if they're dangerous?"

"They're not dangerous," I said for the umpteenth time. "They're angry. Most of the people I know are angry."

Mona gave me a long, thoughtful look. "You know, I'm thinking this class might be just what you need. You've been angry for a long time."

"I've been frustrated," I said.

"No, Kate, you've been angry."

"Okay, whatever. Let's just go."

She started the Jag and put it in gear. We pulled into the rear of the parking lot beside a pickup truck with a gun rack. Mona and I exchanged looks.

Ruth had told me to enter through a heavy wooden door at the back of the church. Mona followed me inside. We passed through a dining room with a dozen long tables. A blackboard announced an upcoming potluck dinner.

I found the stairs leading to the basement. "Be careful," I warned Mona as we started down the tall, narrow flight. It was an old church—the stone walls were worn smooth, the steps badly scuffed. There was an earthy smell. We reached the basement. The paint on the concrete floor had long since faded.

Eight people—five men and three women—had arranged their chairs in a circle and were chatting amongst themselves. On the wall behind them was a large glass-framed painting of Jesus holding a lamb; overhead, a small light shone down on it.

The people stopped talking and gave Mona and me an odd look.

"Who are you?" an older man with a grizzled beard asked. His head was completely bald and as shiny as a new appliance.

I smiled at the group. "I'm Dr. Kate Holly," I said. "Ruth Melvin had an emergency and asked me to take over for her. This is my assistant, Mona Epps."

"What kind of emergency?" The question came

from a middle-aged man in a business suit. "Is she okay?"

I thought it an odd question from somebody who was supposed to be pissed off at the world. "A family illness," I said.

He got up and retrieved two chairs from a number of folded ones leaning against the wall. The group widened their circle as he unfolded them, making room for Mona and me. We thanked him and sat down.

"Just so you know, you're late," a male voice said. I turned toward him. He wore dark slacks and a blue work shirt with the name "Hal's Tires" stitched above his left pocket.

"Shut up, Hal," an elderly woman said, her voice reminding me of my aunt Lou, who smoked non-filtered cigarettes. Her voice was as rough as burlap. The woman had a walker within arm's reach. A large handbag had been tied to the handrail with a scarf.

Mona and I placed our purses beneath our chairs. I glanced at the wall clock not far from the painting of Jesus. Six thirty-five. "Perhaps we could quickly go around the group and introduce ourselves," I said. "If there is anything you'd like to share, feel free."

Nobody moved. Dead silence. I watched the minute hand on the wall clock make a full rotation.

"You first," one of the men said, leaning back in his chair, arms crossed.

I blinked. "Excuse me?"

"You come in here expecting us to spill our guts," he said. "Maybe you should tell us a little about yourself. I kinda get the impression you're not too happy."

"Shut up, Larry," the elderly woman said.

Mona looked at me. "He's right, Kate. This would be a perfect opportunity to unload all your pent-up hostility."

I felt my jaw go slack. "I don't feel hostile."

Mona shrugged. "Okay, stay in denial."

My face felt hot. I shot her a dark look. Mona had been watching Dr. Phil for years—she recorded all of his shows—and had become an armchair psychologist. She took careful notes, not only so she could advise my patients behind my back, but because she dreamed that one day I, too, would have a TV show.

I shifted uncomfortably in my seat and clasped my hands together in my lap. "Well, I admit I've been a little annoyed. My husband is a firefighter, and—" I was interrupted by applause from the group. "Thank you," I said. "I'm very proud of him," I added. I decided not to mention we were divorced, that it had sort of been an accident since I'd intended to stop the proceedings. Too complicated.

"Anyway, it's very stressful at times because I know his job is dangerous. In fact, he was injured six weeks ago." The group murmured a sound of sympathy. "I'm happy to say he has fully recovered."

Mona raised her hand. "What Kate probably won't tell you is how she took care of him on top of holding down a full-time job. It wasn't easy for her."

"Is that what made you angry?" a young woman asked.

I shook my head. "No, I was happy to do it. But I sort of hoped we would have more time together. I wasn't counting on every fireman within a twenty-five-mile radius using my house—I mean *our* house—as an after-work meeting place. Believe me; I've picked up my share of beer cans and peanut hulls."

Chuckles from the group. "I'm trying to work through my resentment," I said, "by reminding myself how much my husband loves his work. I'm sure it was hard on him, sitting home day after day. And it meant a lot to him that his buddies cared enough to visit so often. I know it didn't mean he loved me less."

Several heads nodded. Mona beamed.

I took a deep breath and was surprised how much better I felt. "But please," I said. "I don't want to hog the floor. Would someone else like to share?"

A woman who appeared to be in her mid- to late forties slid forward on her chair. She looked nervous. "My name is Sarah-Margaret," she said, voice trembling. "I attend St. Francis, and I heard our church was offering this group. As I've shared with the others, I'm going through a divorce. Nobody in my family gets divorced," she added, "on account of we're all Catholic. But my husband—he's Catholic, too—doesn't seem to care that he's committing a mortal sin by shacking up with some woman half his age. So, yes, I've been very angry."

She pulled a tissue from her purse and dabbed her eyes. "But I finally realized that, like Ruth said, I've only been hurting myself." She shrugged. "That's all I have to say."

"Thank you, Sarah-Margaret," I said gently, giving her a warm smile. "Divorce is hard," I added, since I'd been there. I looked at the man sitting next to her. He was casually but neatly dressed.

"I'm Ben." He gave a small wave. "Also going through a divorce," he said. He gave a rueful smile. "There seems to be a lot of it going around."

It was Hal's turn. "Hal Horton," he said, and pointed to the patch over his pocket. "I own a tire company. Some of my customers can be a real pain in the ass. As long as everything is going well and my customers like their service, I don't hear anything. Most of them don't bother to say thank you, know what I mean? But if somebody is unhappy, they rake me over the coals. I had it out with the last guy who complained."

"He broke the man's nose," the bearded guy said.

Hal frowned at him. "I was getting to that part, okay? How about you mind your own friggin' business and let me tell my story?"

"Could we please not curse?" Sarah-Margaret said. "We are, after all, in the Lord's house."

Hal looked at her as if she had the word *idiot* written on her forehead.

I glanced at the wall clock. Only ten minutes had passed.

"I punched the guy in the nose," Hal said. "He pressed charges. My wife told me to do something about my temper or she was going to hit the road." He paused and stretched. "Anyway, Ruth said we needed to keep a journal and write down what triggers our anger," he added.

"Have you found that helpful?" I asked.

"Yeah," Hal said. "My trigger is bitchy customers." Several people laughed.

I wondered if Hal was serious about the class or merely taking it because his wife had threatened to leave.

After a moment, he shrugged. "I guess I'm most likely to get angry if I'm tired or hungry," he finally admitted.

Sarah-Margaret raised her hand. "I suggested to Hal that he keep protein bars in his desk. Also, I've started walking an hour every day. It has really helped me with stress and fatigue."

Hal gave a grunt. "Sarah-Margaret is our star pupil," he said, sarcasm ringing loud in his tone. "Which is why I wonder how come she keeps coming," he added.

Sarah-Margaret pressed her lips together in irritation. "There's no need to be rude, Hal."

"I think Hal would rather punch people in the nose," the bearded man said.

Hal flipped him off.

"Oh, that's real mature," Larry said. I looked his way. "I'm Larry, as you've probably guessed. I don't feel like sharing tonight."

"That's fine." I chose to ignore Hal's bad behavior. Some people liked being a bully, and I suspected Hal was one of them. If it were my group, I might have tried to work with him, but I admit I was just trying to get to dinner.

The older woman with the walker spoke. "My name is Bea. I think it's real special that you decided to share your personal problems," she said in a tone that suggested otherwise, "but I paid good money for this class, and I'm not interested in hearing about them."

Mona and I exchanged "uh-oh" looks. "And you have every right to feel that way," I said, thinking it best to validate her feelings and move on. She was rough around the edges. Her face was unmade and dotted with age spots. Her gray hair fell to her shoulders in no particular style. She wore a denim dress and tattered white sneakers.

"Would you like to share, Bea?" I asked.

"Yeah. I'm here because my daughter-in-law is a bitch." She indicated the professionally dressed young woman beside her.

"I resent that remark!" the woman said. "How dare you."

Bea shrugged. "You can resent it all you like, Sandra, but you're still a bitch."

Sarah-Margaret raised her hand. "Could we *please* not use foul language in our Father's house?"

"Shut up, you little wimp," Bea said, and looked my way. "I moved in with Sandra and my son six months ago because I've been having trouble getting around. Bad knees," she added. "My daughter-in-law makes my life miserable."

Sandra looked at me. "Trust me; she's fully capable of being miserable on her own. The only reason my husband and I let her move in is because none of her other children would put up with her."

"That's a damn lie!" Bea said, grabbing her walker and pulling herself to her feet. "My kids love me. The *reason* I live with you and Brandon is because you have the biggest house and I don't have to use the stairs."

"Brandon is the poor sucker who lives with them," Larry said, rolling his eyes. "He made them come here because they were driving him up the wall."

Bea ignored him. "And my son is working his ass off trying to pay for that house because my daughter-in-law is selfish and materialistic." She turned to Sandra. "Let me tell you something, young lady. Brandon could have looked under any rock in Atlanta and found somebody better than you."

Sandra bolted to her feet as well and planted her hands on her hips. "Well, I—"

"Hold it!" I said, cutting off Sandra's response. Things were quickly getting out of hand. The two had anger down to a T. It seemed that it was up to me to manage it. "Perhaps it would be a good idea if both of you calmed down and took a deep breath."

"You're rude and obnoxious," Sandra said to Bea, ignoring me. "All you do is watch game shows while Brandon and I support you. Your room is a pigsty. Living with you is like living with Satan's daughter." Sandra looked at me. "She keeps a gun under her pillow, even though she knows Brandon and I don't approve."

"Deep breath!" I said loudly.

"Maybe it's time I let you have a good look at my gun!" Bea said, snatching a pistol from her pocketbook and aiming it at her daughter-in-law.

Fear hit me like a brick. "No!" I yelled, jumping up as everybody in the group ducked. Sandra screamed; Hal was up and running with lightning speed. Mona and I made a mad dive toward Bea, trying to wrestle the gun from her hand. Hal grasped her from behind, and Mona gave her wrist a karate chop. I pulled the pistol free.

Somehow, my finger accidentally hit the trigger, and a deafening shot rang out, followed by the sound of splintering glass.

Sandra ran screaming from the room.

Bea swung her walker hard and its legs slammed against Hal's shins. Ben joined him, trying to restrain the woman who was obviously not as frail as she appeared.

"Oh, my God!" Sarah-Margaret screamed at me. "You shot Jesus!"

I glanced over my shoulder. The large picture of Jesus holding the lamb lay shattered on the floor.

Sarah-Margaret crossed herself. "This is bad," she said. "This is really bad."

I didn't have time to think about it. "Somebody call nine-one-one!" I shouted, and saw several people reaching for their cell phones.

Sarah-Margaret cradled what was left of the portrait and sobbed hysterically. "Did you see that!" she demanded of the group. "She shot Jesus!"

The man with the beard fell to his knees and began praying.

I dropped the gun and sank onto my chair, my own knees no longer able to support me. I suspected I was going to miss dinner.

"Charlotte Hughes has a million-dollar voice.
Her words turn to gold on the page."
—Janet Evanovich

NEW YORK TIMES BESTSELLING AUTHOR
Charlotte Hughes

What Looks Like Crazy

**The life of a psychologist is enough
to drive anyone nuts…**

Psychologist Kate Holly's life has become the stuff of intensive therapy. She's divorcing her gorgeous firefighter husband, her mother is always meddling, and her psychiatrist ex-boyfriend won't stop calling to find out what color panties she's wearing. Now, Kate's being bombarded with mysterious threats, and the only person who can help her is the one man who always makes her lose her mind—and her heart.

penguin.com

M341T0908

Discover Romance

berkleyjoveauthors.com

See what's coming
up next from your
favorite romance
authors and
explore all
the latest
Berkley,
Jove, and
Sensation
selections.

Fall in love

- See what's new
- Find author appearances
- Win fantastic prizes
- Get reading recommendations
- Chat with authors and other fans
- Read interviews with authors you love

berkleyjoveauthors.com

M1G0907

Penguin Group (USA) Online

What will you be reading tomorrow?

Tom Clancy, Patricia Cornwell, W.E.B. Griffin,
Nora Roberts, William Gibson, Robin Cook,
Brian Jacques, Catherine Coulter, Stephen King,
Dean Koontz, Ken Follett, Clive Cussler,
Eric Jerome Dickey, John Sandford,
Terry McMillan, Sue Monk Kidd, Amy Tan,
John Berendt…

You'll find them all at
penguin.com

*Read excerpts and newsletters,
find tour schedules and reading group guides,
and enter contests.*

Subscribe to Penguin Group (USA) newsletters
and get an exclusive inside look
at exciting new titles and the authors you love
long before everyone else does.

PENGUIN GROUP (USA)
us.penguingroup.com

M224G1107